The Scottish Agent

Book 1: 1789

A Novel by Julie MP Adams

Copyright 2022 Julie MP Adams

The moral right of JMP Adams to be identified as the author of this work has been asserted in accordance with the Copyright, Designs and Patents Act, 1988.

All rights reserved. No part of this publication may be reproduced or transmitted in any form or by any means, electronic or mechanical without permission in writing from the publisher.

This book is a work of fiction. Names, characters, businesses, organizations, places and events are either the product of the author's imagination or used fictitiously. Any resemblance to actual persons, living or dead, events or locales is entirely coincidental.

ISBN: 9798365909007

Other novels by Julie MP Adams

The Lapidary
Malbister
Into the Woods
Broken Wings

Never did anyone do so much harm trying to do so much good

To my grandmother Margaret—with thanks

Character List

Jacob Rose
Johnny Rose (Jacques)
Jeannie Rose (Jean)
Lucette
Sandy Geddes
Francine Geddes
Henriette, sister of Francine
Suzanne Gregoire
Jules, father of Lucette
Gianfranco Valenti
Ottilie de Saint Combs
Cargill, a sea captain

Chapter One

April 9th, 1789

Daylight has faded and with the shutters closed, the public room is lit by the logs in the fireplace and by tallow candles stuck in holders and set on each table, which send shadows scurrying into the dark corners. The tables were scrubbed this morning, and a whiff of lemon and salt has survived the day. At seven of the clock regular customers shuffle in from work and Lucette counts the heads and tells her mother how many souls must be fed from the pot. Legumes are dumped into the stew, loaves of bread set to warm and she returns to the noise and bustle, to fetch tankards and goblets and pour red wine or ale. The more the diners imbibe, the less space in their stomachs for supper. Lucette and her parents eat after the paying customers, from what is left.

In the most fashionable parts of Paris, closer to the Tuileries or the Jardins de Luxembourg, there's a new way to eat—if you have the money. Restaurants, lit by chandeliers, that offer meals several courses long, with even a choice of dishes. The sort of food the aristocrats eat at Versailles.

Lucette can only imagine a place where you can see what's on the plate in front of you. She can only imagine new dresses and shoes of soft leather, never mind the jewels and hair ornaments you'd need to enter such establishments.

Not that this tavern, Le Deux Lions, tucked in a side street close to the Seine, is a poor place. Flames lick the logs in the open fireplace, sending sparks into the air and filling the low-ceilinged room with pine, even though the April evening is mild. Most of the men, and the two women who sit around the tables are bourgeois—soberly dressed, but in clothes that have never been worn by someone else. Lucette's dress is an old one, inherited from an aunt who died last year. Even the muslin *fichu* round her bosom is darned. It has wear left in it, but sometimes she catches a whiff of her aunt's musky scent. She runs her hands over her hips, caressing the starched threadbare cotton How would she feel if she knew that her aunt was the third woman to wear this costume?

Lucette's childhood friend, Marie, is a laundrymaid at Versailles. She wears a pretty dress—of crisp starched striped cotton. She sleeps in an attic dormitory in the Grand Commune and has friends among the army of servitors that feed and dress the nobility. She has prospects and even though she is a skivvy, she gets a glimpse of life at Court.

Lucette's father, Jules, *le patron*, circulates to have a word with the regulars. He puts an arm round one man, smiles at the middle-aged lady who sits with another, and expresses sympathy for two veterans at the table closest to the fire. Antoine and Charles fought in the American Independence Wars with Lafayette. They talk about the rebels and how their comrades fighting against the Redcoats are better off than the people of France. The Americans have elected a President—George Washington, and there's a bright new city being planned. They have rights that the people of

The Scottish Agent

France can barely dream of. Antoine lost fingers in the war, and Charles suffers pain from an old bullet wound that hasn't healed well. These days they are in the military reserves and their pay does not go far.

Charles could seek help from Doctor Jean Paul Marat, sitting at the next table, he thinks, but the doctor shakes his head and tells him these days he writes about science and politics. He doesn't practice medicine anymore. Marat is not a regular customer. His health is poor, and to be honest, Lucette worries that his skin condition might be catching. On some days, the poor man can hardly leave his bed, but this evening, he has come to dine with friends.

At the table in the centre of the room, she fills the cup of the Scotsman, Monsieur Rose. He's always known as the *Ecossaise*, although he hasn't lived in Scotland since he was a child. His French is excellent, and there are many who seek his advice. He can turn his hand to drawing up a contract or a Will, and the merchants who struggle to import goods get his young clerk to draft their documents. They've needed his help. 1788 was a hot and dry year, and to add to the drought, the great hailstorm of 14th July ruined the harvest. Lucette was on an errand that day. She had gone to buy some ribbons and wore her best dress for the outing. She remembers the bright sun swallowed by a monstrous blanket of clouds, and how she was flung on her face on the cobbled road, hands over her head as the lumps of ice, each the size of a cherry, hammered her. She eventually picked herself up and when she reached home, soaked and shivering, and stripped to her shift, she was covered in bruises.

Lucette's parents worry about money. She knows that they discuss it when they are in bed, with the candle snuffed out. As the cost of grain rises, and a few *sous* are added to each loaf or each plate, they struggle to break even. She hears her father moan to Doctor Marat about the taxes he must pay. Half of every day's profits go in revenue, as is the case for everyone who is not a member of the clergy or an aristocrat. Those taxes paid for the foreign wars and they keep the King and court in comfort at Versailles. Many a peasant or shopkeeper reflects they have never seen the Hall of Mirrors or the Queen's little farm at Trianon, but their money pays for those luxuries.

The Scotsman corresponds with his home country. He writes to Adam Smith and Thomas Muir. He pens missives to James MacPherson about poetry, and copies of the latest books arrive by the case at his modest home. He talks of an Enlightenment in philosophy, economics and politics. He has a copy of Thomas Paine's 'Common Sense' hidden in his bookshelves. He raises his glass to Doctor Marat and tells him news of mutual friends at St Andrews university. Scotland and France have long been friends, and the new ideas interest men of letters in both countries.

Finally, food is ready, and Lucette and her father collect pewter plates laden with today's stew and bring them to the table. The food smells of garlic and wine; is nourishing and there's enough to fill empty tummies, but the mutton was on the turn. Maman hopes the diners will not notice. Lucette serves the Scotsman and his clerk, a pale young man who looks too young to shave. The latter gives her a nod and asks for his cup to be refilled. She goes to fetch the ale jug. In the kitchen, her mother looks up, and twitches Lucette's cap and *fichu*. Satisfied her daughter looks presentable, she pushes her back out to collect empty plates, and look for a husband. Lucette is almost nineteen and she should be married by now. For the moment, she earns her keep as the waitress, but as times grow increasingly hard, she is a mouth they might not be able to afford to feed.

The men who dine here are regulars. They have houses and are men of business but have no wives or servants to cook for them. Some are widowers, like the shopkeeper, Mercier, who sits by the window. His wife died in childbirth three years ago, and behind his back, Lucette's mother says it is high time he found another. Lucette collects his half empty plate. She knows he won't notice her until the day he finishes his food and forgets to sigh. His wife was two years older than Lucette.

One of the women diners summons Lucette to refill her cup, and they exchange a few words. Lucette has never seen the lady before, but she can tell from the rings on her fingers and the quality of her *fichu*, that she is wealthier than their usual customers. The woman offers a tip and Lucette accepts it with a smile, tucking the coins into the pocket she wears under her petticoat.

Several new customers have come in to sit with Doctor Marat. One young man with ink-stained fingers talks nineteen to the dozen. His voice is angry, and Marat gestures to him to calm down. Lucette moves closer to try to hear the conversation properly, but her father hands her some empty plates and sends her back to the kitchen, while he sits down with them and talks of things that could land a man in the Bastille. Lucette hopes they won't be too indiscreet. One of those young men has been paying her compliments when she takes her walk, and she likes the feeling of being courted by a young, good-looking man. He looks round and gives her a conspiratorial wink. She blushes, but a warmth spreads through her body.

She loves Papa, and she doesn't want him to get into trouble. Her admirer is looking across at the Scotsman's clerk, who lowers his head and refuses to greet him.

There is always talk. Talk of extravagance at court. Talk of America. Talk of a better life. Now the talk is getting louder. There are rumours. After over a hundred and fifty years, the King in his gilded cage is summoning the Three

Estates. He has no choice in the matter. There's no money in the Treasury. Change is coming.

Chapter Two

Supper over, the Scotsman and his clerk pay Jules in coin, bid their fellow diners good night, gather their coats and set out for home. This part of the city has streetlights—candle lanterns hung over the roads and paid for by *taxe des boues et des lanternes* . It has rained and puddles on the cobbled streets reflect the lights above.

Jacob Alexander Rose carries a staff—a tall walking stick, that conceals a weapon—a slim blade that he isn't afraid to use if they are set upon by footpads. Few would try. He's not a big man—but he walks everywhere, carries himself well and doesn't look so prosperous that he would be a target for footpads. His suit of clothes, like those of all the middle classes of Paris is made of plain dark wool—silks and satins are reserved for the nobility. He carries a silver timepiece, but it is concealed inside a plain waistcoat. He doesn't powder his hair or wear a wig—his dark hair is plaited and clubbed with a plain ribbon. He makes a virtue of being inconspicuous. In a crowd you would find it hard to pick him out, and he likes it that way.

The clerk, Jean, slinks at his back, laden with a bulging

satchel. His suit does not fit his narrow frame well. It is old and belonged to the lad's father, dead these past five years. His light brown hair is worn tied back in the same way as his employer, but he has an outmoded tricorn hat, worn low over his eyes.

They pass a church. Easter is next week, and it is lit up. The door opens and a woman emerges, richly dressed. The priest is at the door, and the light catches the gold embroidery on the stole over his white surplice. He exchanges words with the lady but is blind to the beggars sleeping on the steps.

The clerk comments on the injustice. The church pays no taxes, and those who hold rank are from the nobility. He doesn't think there is anything noble about them. In Scotland, times are hard, but the Church of Scotland would take a dim view of beggars left to starve outside the Kirk.

They reach home, opening the iron gate that leads into a tiny courtyard. Rose puts his key into the lock, turns it and pushes the door open. He crosses to the fireplace, where the embers are still glowing and adds some coal. When the flames stir, he lights the candles on the mantelpiece. The mirror doubles the candlelight, and the room becomes visible, as the beams bounce off light painted walls. He motions to Jean to close the shutters.

'Do you need me to work this evening?' the clerk asks.

Rose shakes his head. 'I have some letters to write, Jean. Take yourself off to your bed, lad. You look tired.'

The boy bends to the embers with a paper spill and lights a half-used candle in a metal holder before climbing the bare wooden stairs to his attic.

It's a modest house and the room where Jacob Rose pours himself a glass of Madeira and settles in his chair behind the desk is his place of business as well as his private sitting room. There's one room on each of four floors. The basement has the scullery where a laundrymaid works one day a week to wash their linen in the copper. No public *lavoir* for the Rose men. Above the office is his bedchamber—a plain space with a small bed, a commode and a press to hold his clothes. He managed fine enough on his own, until an upturn in business demanded he hire a clerk. Jean is quiet as a mouse, and most of the time he hardly notices the boy is there at all, as he sits at the window desk and makes copies of documents in a round, fair hand.

Now, Jacob reaches for a goose feather quill, and trims it with the penknife before dipping it into the silver inkwell. This letter requires thought. In the tavern, he heard news that worries him. In America things are making progress. Washington's election and forthcoming inauguration is good news for the Americans. It will be well received by Lafayette—but those former soldiers tonight are not alone in now wanting change for France.

The Three Estates—or Estates General represent three groups in French society. Each has only one vote. The First Estate—the Church holds considerable power and is immensely rich. The most important clergy are nobles. The Second Estate—the Nobility—includes not only ancient dukedoms, but also those men of business who bought their place at Versailles during the reign of the last three Louis. It's a good investment—it brings immunity from paying taxes. That means the Third Estate—the largest of all, can always be outvoted by the other two. The Third Estate bears the weight of all the taxation in the country. It includes everyone from those beggars on the church steps to the shopkeeper Mercier; to bankers; to lawyers like young Maximillian Robespierre and to doctors and scientists like Marat.

Now that the Americans have shown the way, how long before Civil War breaks out in France?

Jacob Rose knows what wars do. He was born in the

Julie MP Adams

Northeast of Scotland thirty-two years ago, to parents whose fortunes never recovered from the '45 Rebellion. Their clan chief—a canny man who entertained the Bonnie Prince four nights before Culloden and welcomed Butcher Cumberland on the evening after the battle—hedged his bets and avoided sequestration. The old alliance between France and Scotland—which existed centuries before the 1707 Union—is a hard habit to break, especially for those with a taste for the finer things in life, like claret and cognac. The Rose family found it convenient to have an agent in Paris, as they dabbled in trade and politics. Now that Jacob's father is dead, the duty falls to him. The lady laird of Kilravock and the factor who manages her estates, have friends in government, including George Rose, the joint secretary to the Treasury, who has the ear of Pitt and Jacob knows the letter he writes will find its way to Henry Dundas, a man with political ambitions who all but rules Scotland these days.

He writes swiftly, covering the page with a fluent copperplate, and few crossings out. He doesn't bother with a cipher—the sea captain, Cargill, from the port of Arbroath, is in Paris, with his ship docked at Le Havre. He's brought sugar and molasses from Martinique and will collect brandy and silk to deliver to Leith on his way home. This letter will be in a package of other correspondence Rose will hand him for their man of business in Edinburgh.

He signs the page, dusts it with sand, and once satisfied the ink is dry, he folds the paper and seals it, pushing his signet ring with the family crest—a harp with an angel and the legend Constant and True—into the dark red wax. He picks up the oiled silk bag with the other letters and adds this one before locking it into the desk and putting the key in his waistcoat pocket.

He checks the fire is safe before taking the candle and climbing the stairs to his bed.

Chapter Three

April 10th, 1789

The next morning is rainy, and the sun sullenly refuses to break through heavy clouds. By eight o clock, Jacob is at his desk, quill in hand and ledger open. The clerk has cleared away the breakfast bowls of chocolate and the plate of brioche he fetched from the baker at dawn.

Jean scowls as he returns to his high perch at the window. Not that there's much to be seen in the tiny courtyard. But the bell at the gate is rung, and Cargill—a leather skinned seadog—tramps into the office. He has the gait of a pack pony, but his sharp grey eyes miss nothing.

He greets Jean with a nod, and a curious look. Jean bobs his head in greeting but returns to his work.

'How's the lad doing?' Cargill asks.

Jacob indicates a seat, and Cargill sits, extending a stiff leg as he does so.

'Jean's a good help,' Jacob replies. 'Can we offer you some refreshment? A dish of tea? A glass of ale?'

Cargill accepts the ale, although it is still early. Jacob

directs Jean to fill the copper kettle, which he hangs over the coals. It's too early for him to drink alcohol and he'd rather like a cup of tea.

Cargill rummages in his pack and produces an oilskin bag, which he shoves across the table to Jacob. 'The Fortuna docked in Le Havre, just after us and I said I'd deliver the post for his captain. He's eager to get on to Algiers.'

Jacob unlocks the drawer and hands over his own package. 'Get this to Riddell in Leith, for me—it could be urgent.'

Cargill grunts and stows the bag into his pack. 'You're expecting trouble?'

Jacob nods and crosses the room to lift the kettle off the hook, setting it on the hearth as he unlocks the tea caddy and spoons the precious contents into the silver pot. Tea is his luxury, served in the English way, and he pours the hot water over the leaves, and lets it brew, before pouring it into a delicate, thin bone china cup, decorated in azure blue and gold. It's Sevres, and a gift from one of his wealthier clients. He alone washes this cup, which is too precious to trust to the laundry girl, or even to Jean, who can be clumsy.

Rummaging again in his pack, Cargill produces other packages—tobacco, sugar loaf, and a bag of coffee beans. Jacob accepts them, and hands over coins in payment.

'How was your voyage?' he asks. 'Any excitement on the way?'

The sea captain produces a pipe and proceeds to fill it from a leather pouch. He takes a paper spill from a jar on the hearth and takes his time to light it, and then the pipe. He puffs for a minute, before answering. 'The usual. I had a full hold of poor souls from Guinea to Saint Domingue, and we lost a quarter of them on the way to scurvy and the flux. It took a week to wash out the hold and load the cargo. We had business in America, so we detoured and docked off Boston, and I sent a boat in with letters for Kilravock's man.'

'What do you make of the rebels?'

'Let's just say that we should all go and be Americans, lad. We can talk all we like of freedom, but they've managed to grab theirs. Could you imagine the like of that in Scotland? Nae kings or lords—but elections and new ideas. I'd go there the morn, if it wasn't for the wife and her kin.'

Cargill's wife is the daughter of a mill owner who makes the Osnaburg cloth the poor Caribbean slaves wear, and whose other mill produces the sails for his ship. He was content with crossing the North Sea to collect flax from the Baltic, but his wife's family have pushed him to sail the black triangle and be more directly connected to the slave trade. Jacob senses the man is bone weary of the cruelty.

Cargill nods at the letters he's delivered, as he heaves himself to his feet. 'I came here first, but I've errands to run for Kilravock and for the wife's father. If you've got time to read those and you need to reply, I can collect them before I go back to the ship tomorrow.'

Jacob is already breaking the seal and reading. He glances up and asks where Cargill will be staying the night?

'I've got a bed at Sandy Geddes' house. It means I must suffer through dinner with the family—unless...?' he looks up.

Jacob smiles. 'I shall see fit to call on your hosts this evening. After dinner, around seven?'

Cargill has a busy day ahead—he must place orders for wine and for silk and deliver the special cargoes that Geddes—a wealthy man whose French wife has connections at court—has commissioned. One of those cargoes, a lad of about ten years, is shivering on the cart outside. It's fashionable to have a blackamoor page, and the lad will be pampered—until he grows too tall and broad to be a pet.

At the window, Jean watches Cargill depart. He too was

a special cargo—brought from Aberdeen to Paris, to be the clerk to the older Rose—who is every bit as much of a servant as he is.

Jean has taken to smuggling some of the more radical books upstairs. He's been reading Thomas Paine and keeping his ears cocked at the inn for the conversation of those who want better and want it to happen soon. He finds it odd that despite the radical nature of the books on his master's shelf—and his bonhomie towards the likes of Marat, that Jacob refuses to engage in conversation on what is doubtless about to happen.

Chapter Four

Lunch at the *Deux Lions* is a simple affair. A bowl of soup, a piece of bread and a chunk of cheese, washed down with a glass of red. The bread is always fresh, if expensive and in short supply these days, and the cheese sent from the countryside, where Jules' brother-in-law farms a smallholding. Jacob enjoys his noontime walk—a break from his endeavours, and it's often the only daylight young Jean sees.

Today, Jules is morose and monosyllabic, and his wife flutters around the kitchen in tears, with the hem of her apron dabbed to reddened eyes. Lucette is nowhere to be seen.

Jean has been looking round anxiously. Jacob suspects he has feelings for the lass. She's young and comely, and even in that old, darned frock, she is a ray of sunlight. Without her, the tavern is dismal.

Jules serves the soup—his wife following with the bread and cheese. Unlike Lucette's graceful dance around the common room, her mother, still red eyed and upset, must take her time. Jacob wants to know what has happened, but he waits until service is over and asks Jules to take wine with him. The man brings the jug and an extra cup and pours with a shaking hand.

'Is Lucette unwell?' Jean asks, earning a glare from his employer and a swift kick to the shins under the table.

'She's gone,' Jules replies, taking a drink. He sets the cup down with a clatter.

'My friend—what has happened?' Jacob asks. Jules has had several cups of wine, by the looks of it and his hands are shaking.

'Last night, after you left, my landlord came in. He gave notice that our lease has expired and if we wish to renew it, the rent will go up. We could barely afford what we were paying before, but now?'

Over the past quarter century, incomes rose by a fifth—but prices and rents rose by three times as much. For a man like Jules, with half his profits taxed, a rent rise could mean ruin, Jacob reflects.

'How does this affect the lass?' he asks.

'We've always known she couldn't stay here much longer, but we hoped to find her a husband. In fact, my wife had hoped...'

'I'm not in a position to support a wife or a family, and Jean here certainly can't,' he says. 'Where's she gone?'

'Lucette's best friend, Marie Galant, is a servant at Versailles. She was on a visit home—her father died and the funeral was yesterday. Lucette asked her to help her find a place months ago. She packed her things and left this morning. My wife is heartbroken.'

'It's hard when she's your only one,' Jacob commiserates.

The man nods and leans forward. 'She wasn't ours to keep. The lease on this place was our payment for taking her. Not that anyone remembers now.'

Lucette's mother's marriage prospects were ruined by the

birth of the child. The father—a music master with talent that didn't match his charm and appearance, was despatched by *lettre de cache*t to prison, and the mother packed off to take the veil in a closed order. The baby was an inconvenience, until it was suggested the third footman and kitchen maid, who wanted to leave service and marry, might adopt her and raise her as their own.

'God didn't grant us any children, so we were glad of her. Lucette doesn't know any of this, and if my wife knew I'd told anyone, it would break her heart. We arrived here as man and wife with a baby daughter, and that's all anyone needed to know.'

Jacob exchanges a glance with Jean, who nods understanding.

'Jules, she will be with other girls her age, and they'll feed and clothe her. Perhaps you need to be happy for her. The court servants eat better than most folk in Paris. If it's of any help, I have business from time to time at Versailles. I can get a message to her, and bring a reply, just to reassure you.'

Jacob pays for lunch and counts out an extra coin.

They are walking home when Jean says, 'I don't think the servants are all well treated. I hear rumours.'

Jacob stops and the look he gives Jean is an icy dagger. 'I'm fully aware of what goes on at Versailles, lad. But not a word of that to the poor man back there. He's breaking his heart already. Do you want to kill him with grief?'

He takes two paces and then stops and turns. 'Where exactly have you been hearing rumours?'

Has Jean been going out at night, when he claims to be in his attic, reading? And what company is he keeping?

Jean says, 'When we get home, I'll show you.'

The pamphlets are little more than scandal sheets. Jacob has seen them before and he knows their purpose is to stir up hatred of the queen, Marie Antoinette.

'Where did you get these?' he asks, but already knows—those inky fingered agitators who are never far from Marat. He noticed one of them trying to catch Jean's eye in the tavern last night.

Jean is so quiet he hardly says boo to a goose, but Jacob knows the quiet ones are often the most dangerous. He will need to keep a closer eye on his clerk.

Chapter Five

A messenger arrives in the afternoon with an invitation for Jacob to dine with the Geddes family. It doesn't extend to Jean, who will eat as usual chez Jules, but with strict instructions to return home early and continue his work. The lad's been too distracted to concentrate, since he learned of Lucette's departure.

Jacob goes upstairs to freshen up and change. He has hired a Sedan chair for the evening, so he puts on shoes with fancier buckles and his coat is a finer wool with dark coloured silk embroidery. Jean has not yet returned, so he leaves the key on the lintel for him.

The Geddes house is in the Rue du Faubourg St Honore, close to the Louvre. It is well lit, and as he alights from the chair, he notices the flaming torches at both sides of the door.

Francine Geddes fancies herself as a *salonnniere*, much to her husband's amusement. Her heroine, Olympe de Gouges would be horrified by Cargill's special cargo. As an opponent of slavery, and an advocate of the rights of women, de Gouges is known to ruin the social prospects of anyone who keeps a house slave.

Francine and Sandy are excellent hosts, however, and Benjamin Franklin was a regular face at their table, while he was resident in Paris. They strike a balance of the wealthier bourgeoisie, some dissident nobles, foreign diplomats and occasional merchants and traders. Tonight, they are dining *en famille*, and all the guests are Scots, or married to them. Besides Cargill and Jacob is a banker who lives several doors away, Francis Macdonald and his wife, Marie.

Sandy, a bluff man who is tall and broad, and has never really lost his Scottishness, greets Jacob warmly, and steers him towards the fireplace where Cargill is holding court, with tales of his voyages. The page is beside him, beautifully dressed in a velvet livery that Jacob recognises as that of a senior courtier's household. His host follows his gaze and says, 'The lad will be off to Versailles tomorrow. His new master will send a conveyance for him first thing.'

'He's very young. What's Cargill told you of him?'

'He bought him in San Domingue. He's about ten years old, and he speaks perfect French and passable English. His mother was a house slave, and from all accounts, her master used her as his bed companion as well as his cook. The master died and the son and his wife sold her and the lad—who might well have been his half-brother, to get them out of the way. The lad's called Etienne, and when he was ripped from her, she tried to throw herself into the harbour. Smart little fellow ordered her to keep herself safe. Told her that he would come back and take care of her. His masters would do well to watch him—he might be young, but he sees everything. He told my wife last night that the cook has been selling our left-over bread at the back door.'

Jacob raises his eyebrows. 'Isn't that common practice?'

Sandy shrugs— 'Seemingly in San Domingue, a servant would be whipped for it. I'd have expected a bit of solidarity with my household, but that wee lad has his own agenda. I've told Francine to watch what she says when he's around.' He catches his wife's eye and she approaches them. In contrast to her husband's bulk, Francine is barely five feet tall, and despite her fashionably styled hair, she barely comes up to his shoulder. She is an exotic bird, in her peacock blue dress, with peacock side feathers in her hair. She might be a merchant's wife, but her ways are those of the Court.

The dining room is beautifully lit by beeswax candles in paired sconces fastened to mirrors around the room. There are candles in ornate silver gilt holders on the table, and each place is set with gleaming silver cutlery and delicately engraved glasses. Light dances around every surface, suffusing the room in a golden glow.

Jacob takes his place and opens the lace edged linen napkin, flapping it into place on his lap.

The food, as always, is delicious. Sandy and Francine keep an excellent table. The soup, delicately light, is chicken, and the main course is poached pheasant with seasonal vegetables. Jacob is cutting into his meat, when Sandy asks after his clerk.

'I beg your pardon,' Jacob says, dabbing his mouth with the napkin. 'Did you wish me to bring him this evening?'

'No—but I did want to find out how the lad is settling in. When I wrote to Aberdeen to find you an apprentice, there was some concern about him.'

'Really?' Jacob replies, taking up his knife and fork again, 'Jean is so quiet I hardly know he's there. He's a hard worker. I've left him copying documents for Cargill's homeward voyage.'

'There was a bit of fuss over some of the company he'd been keeping. His guardian thought a change of scenery would do the lad and his sister good. Tell me, has he been to see her at all?'

Jacob chews on his meat, wanting so much to concentrate on the tender fillet, and the jus around it, but now unable to enjoy it. 'I didn't even know he has a sister. If I ask him about home, it seems to upset him and we change the subject.' He takes another forkful, but before he guides it to his mouth, he sets it down and asks, 'What do you know about him—and his sister?'

Sandy takes a drink from his wine glass before saying, 'They're twins, Johnnie and Jeannie Rose. Their mother died giving birth to them, and their father took a new wife when they were about twelve. They were sent to bide with an uncle, a kirk minister in Aberdeen, who took in young folk to educate them, to get them ready for the university. Normally it would just have been the lad, but the two were inseparable, and the lass didn't get on with her stepmother, so it was suggested she would share the lessons and be a companion for the minister's daughter.'

Jacob says, 'Where's the concern? It sounds as if they had a good enough start in life.'

Sandy nods, raises a forkful of meat to his mouth, and chews with obvious enjoyment. 'Their father died five years ago, and the stepmother refused to leave the house, and forbade either of them to return to live with her. The minister kept them under his roof while the lad was at the university, but the funds to support them dried up, and he told them they'd need to find another patron or find employment. When I wrote, their names were put forward: the lad as your clerk and the lass as a companion for old Mistress Danby, who wanted a girl from Scotland who spoke French. Cargill, here, brought them over seven months ago, but he needed to catch the tide, and they came from Le Havre to Paris on the public conveyance.'

Marie Macdonald, across the table, has been listening. 'Was that Georgina Danby you were talking about?'

Sandy, mopping up the jus with a piece of bread, raises his head, 'Aye, the same.'

'Georgina Danby died back in September,' Francis replies. 'I had to read the lesson at her funeral. There was no young companion servant present.'

Jacob looks blank. 'What's become of the lass? Her brother hasn't asked for help for her. Might they have friends in Paris we don't know about?'

Sandy frowns. 'If they have, its highly likely they're the wrong sort of folk. There was another reason the twins came to Paris. It was to stop the lad being transported to Australia as a felon. They can't go home.'

CHAPTER SIX

Jean goes to *Le Deux Lions* as usual. Without Lucette, it is a dismal place. The stew tonight has more legumes and lentils than meat, and he finds it hard to digest. He drinks his ale and avoids looking at the other diners.

Jean finishes, paying with the coins Jacob handed him before he went out. He has a long evening of work ahead, and he's tired. The headache that has plagued him all day has not lifted and all he really wants to do is go to his bed. On his solitary walk homeward, he hears footsteps behind him, and stops, turning to look, but seeing nobody.

At the door, he puts his hand up on the lintel for the key that Jacob will have left there but doesn't find it. Then he realises that there is light within. There's an intruder.

He pushes the door open, nervously.

There's a young man sitting in Jacob's chair, drawn up to the fire. He has helped himself to a glass of Madeira and to a biscuit from the tin that Jacob keeps with the bottle. He looks completely at home, one leg crossed casually over the other. 'Hello, sister mine. No word of welcome?' His hand around the glass has ink-stained fingers.

The Scottish Agent

'Who saw you come in, Johnny? And what do you want this time?' The words are polite, but there is vinegar in Jean's voice. The papers on the desk, the same papers that Cargill delivered earlier, are open and weighted down by the pebble that Jacob keeps as a memento of his birthplace on the Nairn coast. She's sure that Jacob put them away in the leather folder and put the folder in the drawer of the desk.

'It's always good to keep up with the news, Jeannie. Besides, I want to know what's going on in Scotland.'

The likeness is strong, although Johnny is two inches taller. They have the same blue-grey eyes; the same straight noses; the same thin upper lip, and the same light brown hair. They share the same small-boned frame, but there's a hardness to the boy's features and a cynicism to his voice.

'How is your arrangement going, sister?' Johnny is helping himself to another glass of Madeira, and she snatches the bottle away.

'He marks it—you'll get me in trouble.'

Jean or Jeannie puts the bottle away in the cupboard, and crosses to stir the fire and add coals. She lights the candles, but then she takes a seat over to the fire, and puts her head in her hands, wearily.

'I'm sick of this. I spend hours at that wee desk over by the window, ruining my eyesight, copying out documents. The only time I get off is a walk to the baker to get the bread, and the meals at that miserable wee tavern. The only peace I get is when I can get up to my attic, with half a candle. The man's a skinflint. He watches every bloody penny. It's no wonder he hasn't got a wife.'

'Has he paid you?' Johnny is sitting up to attention. She might have guessed he wouldn't be here out of concern for her welfare.

She shakes her head. 'He pays me bed and board, and there'll be three gold pieces in September for me. Will that be enough for your passage?'

He shrugs. 'I might have decided that I want to stick around for the time being. It looks like there's going to be changes.'

'Monsieur Marat tells you that?' she replies.

This is not what they agreed.

From childhood, Johnny has always been the lively one—the mischief maker. He cheeked their stepmother, Flora, and their father, Jamie, in exasperation, sent him to the Reverend Robert Milne, in Aberdeen, to be educated. The minister was a hard taskmaster, but he failed to notice how much of the actual studying was done by Jeannie, and how little Johnny did. By the time the university place began, Johnny would spend his nights sneaking out to make mischief and sleep through the following morning. Jeannie, in her brother's spare clothes, attended the lectures, handing the notes to her brother in time for him to go to his tutorials in the afternoon, while she took her place with the minister's wife and daughter, sewing or working in the garden. When night fell, she would read aloud in the parlour, retiring to bed ostensibly with a headache, to work on the essays that Johnny would later claim as his own.

Johnny was fond of saying he was keeping company with the young Reformers who hung about the university and frequented the ale houses, but he spoke rashly and loudly and drank too much. It was easy for others, when questioned, to point the finger of blame at him, and last July he spent a week in the cells, only released when Jeannie pleaded with the Reverend to speak for him. The University, naturally, sent him down, which meant that Jeannie's own education was also at an end.

Paris was proposed by their benefactor, the lady of Kilravock, as a solution to the problem. Mistress Danby would enjoy Jeannie's company and could introduce her to society where she might even find a husband. Johnny would clerk for Jacob Rose, and if he still wished to be a rebel, he could save up his earnings and take ship for America. She would not divulge his recent behaviour to his new employer—he could begin with a clean slate.

Jeannie fastened her hopes on the old lady and a life where she could have some comforts. Even Johnny, for whom a clerk's life was distasteful, looked forward to a society where the bourgeoisie could openly discuss politics without being thrown in jail or onto a prison ship bound for Australia. Their behaviour on their voyage was impeccable.

Johnny convinced Cargill to let them take the public conveyance to Paris. Dropped with their bags—all their worldly goods—in the Isle de la Cite they made their way by foot to the Danby house, to find it shuttered. The servant at the door broke the news that the lady was dead, and there was no place for Jeannie.

They had little money and no place to stay for the night. It was Johnny's idea to revive their old conspiracy. Jeannie could use their father's old suit to become Jean the clerk, and he would find some employment elsewhere. It was easier for a young man to fend for himself, he argued and besides, Jeannie was far more suited to the drudgery of a clerk, wasn't she?

Seven months of constant work, and little contact with the outside world—but of late, Johnny has been reckless, turning up at the tavern with his printer friend, Le Maitre, to drink with Marat. She must turn her back on him, lest she betray them both.

It's money he's after. It's usually that or finding an alibi for his nocturnal activities.

'Where's Lucette?'

She looks up. 'What's it to you?'

'Her father, Jules, seems to look up to your master.

What's he said?'

Jeannie sighs, 'They've got money worries. The girl's taken a job at Versailles. She's off to be a servant.'

She looks at her brother's face. 'Have you been playing with her feelings?'

She doesn't see the smirk she was expecting. Instead, his face is contorted with pain.

'She's different from the others. Jeannie—I think I'm in love with her.'

Chapter Seven

In Scotland, the ladies would retire to their parlour, to drink a glass of something, and perhaps one of them might read aloud, or they might take up their knitting. The men would take the opportunity to use the chamber pot left discreetly in a corner of the dining room and enjoy a glass of port while they talk of business and politics.

They are not in Scotland. Paris is different and the ladies remain at table. The dishes are cleared and later there will be a hand or two of cards, but for the moment, talk turns to the Assembly that will meet next month at Versailles.

Geddes and Macdonald, having established business interests as well as French wives, are taking a keen interest in affairs. They have clients at court. Francine's sister is wife to a recently ennobled landowner, who controls plantations in the colonies. When there's a demand for small pageboys, she can arrange for their transportation through her sister and brother-in-law. Macdonald's wife, on the other hand, was born noble, the youngest daughter of a widowed Marquise, whose extravagant expenditure at court meant there was no money left for a dowry for all her five daughters. The match is happy enough, even if it began as a business transaction. A wedding ring, and a house in Paris in exchange for an introduction at court for the banker, who now includes dukes and princes among his clients.

Jacob, who works for his host and his neighbour, notarising documents and negotiating trade—a tricky business as technically France neither imports nor exports other than within its own territory, suspects they are concerned for their own affairs.

'Your mother was French, wasn't she, Jacob?' Macdonald says a little too casually, snapping his fingers to the footman to refill his glass with cognac.

'I was born in Scotland,' Jacob reminds him gently, as his own glass is filled and he raises it to his lips.

'You've lived here almost all of your life, though, and you're more of a citizen than either of us,' Geddes remarks. 'You could be nominated as a member of the Third Estate, couldn't you?'

This is the very last thing that Jacob Alexander Rose wants, and he says so. 'There are worthier men than me.'

'Francine tells me that the salons are full of those who are all too willing to take a seat. We need men of reason and ideas. Men of letters—not the likes of Marat and Danton, or that funny little man? What's his name again?'

Francine murmurs 'Maximilien Robespierre.'

He continues, 'Someone needs to have an ear open for the interests of Scotland. If they can effect change here, what's to say those changes couldn't reach across the seas?'

'Those changes in America were dearly bought—why do you think the Treasury here is empty? How many Scottish families lost sons on both sides?' Jacob thinks of a cousin— a major in the King's army, lost in battle, and the man's family, thrown on the mercy of Kilravock for bed and board.

'Besides,' he continues, 'you both do rather well under

the status quo. I don't—why don't you get one of your wealthy merchants to come forward. They'll be better placed to talk about taxes and representation than a poor notary.'

He watches them exchange a glance. Cargill has been quiet throughout the exchange. 'Did you have time to read *all* of your letters?' he asks, puffing at his pipe.

The suggestion has been made by his hosts, but it is an order from Scotland. His heart sinks. He might read the works of Thomas Paine, but his interest is academic—he'd much prefer to keep it so.

His chair arrives later, and on the way home, he thinks of Jules. If he agrees, it will not be for his wealthy friends- and it will not be for his British spymasters: he will go to help people like the innkeeper and his heartbroken wife.

Chapter Eight

Jeannie, thrown off balance by the idea that her twin has a heart, listens to him pour it out for a girl that until today she had dismissed as a servant. She's learned more than she really wants to deal with today. She looks at the clock on the mantelpiece and tells Johnny to leave—unless he is prepared to tell Jacob the truth about their deception. After he goes—she closes the door and sits at the desk, gathering up the papers and replacing them in the leather folder.

She doesn't really intend to look at them, but on the top is a report from Jacob to his patrons in Edinburgh. She knows it needs to be sealed—her brother broke the wax. She scurries up the stairs to her attic, and rummages in the small box that holds her belongings. There's a moment of panic before her fingers close over her father's ring—which she insisted on taking from Johnny.

She slips back down, and at the desk, she folds the paper, committing its contents to memory, holds the stick of wax over the candle flame, and presses the signet into the dark red puddle of wax. She waits for it to cool and harden before replacing it in the folder and shoving the folder back into the desk drawer. Damn—she was sure it was locked. Johnny must have forced the lock and she knows that Jacob always keeps the key on his person.

She takes the glass her brother drank from to the scullery, washes it, and returns it to the cupboard, along with the bottle. If Jacob notices, she will need to say it was her, even though he knows she hardly touches liquor.

She douses all the candles but one, settles the fire and takes her light over to the desk where she must catch up with her work. She is methodical but by now her eyes are tired, and her quill is spitting inkblots on the papers. When the clock chimes nine, she tidies her desk and taking the light in her hand, retreats to her attic.

She closes her shutters, and by the light of the candle, lets her jacket fall, kicks off her shoes and strips off knee breeches and stockings. She unwinds the stock from her neck, and standing in her shirt, she tidies her armour away onto the back of the chair. She pulls the shirt over her head and sniffs at it, before folding it and setting it on the woven rush seat. One garment remains: the modified corset which changes what is a slim girlish figure into that of a slender lad. If she had the figure of Lucette, she could never keep up the pretence of being her own brother. The woefully flat bosom that the Reverend's wife despaired would never attract a husband, is perfectly acceptable if one is acting the part of a nineteen-year-old boy.

In Aberdeen, she had handed Johnny the scissors and instructed him to saw through her plait. The thing hung to her waist, and she would never carry off the pretence without chopping it to below her shoulders. Now, she undoes the ribbon, unplaits her light brown locks and drags a comb through them. She will need to get her hair trimmed again—it's several inches longer than a young man would keep it.

Before her washstand, she pours cold water from the

ewer into the bowl. Dipping a cloth into the water, and rubbing it on the ball of soap, she washes face, underarms and draws the cloth over her arms. Drying herself with the rough towel, she pulls her voluminous nightshirt over her head. She uses a small brush to clean her teeth—with a tooth powder that the apothecary tells her is used at court, although she can only take his word for that. Finally, she pulls back the sheet and slides into bed. The candle gutters and goes out, just as the door downstairs opens. Jacob is home.

She hears him move around the ground floor, locking up before he climbs the stairs to his bedchamber. Tonight, for the first time, he climbs to the attic. She waits for a knock that does not come. Instead, his footsteps retreat down to his room. She realises she has been holding her breath, and lets it go in a deep sigh.

Chapter Nine

Johnny hasn't gone far—he's lurked outside Jacob's house, gathering his thoughts. He's caught a glimpse of his sister, at her little desk, beavering away at the job that technically is his. He doesn't envy her—she has the patience he has always lacked. However, he's convinced Le Maitre and Marat that she is useful, and he learned quite a lot tonight from reading those letters. His fingers close on the device in his pocket: a skeleton key that he used on the desk lock. Perhaps he should have offered to secure it again—Jeannie will need to find an excuse if Jacob notices. It's not as if she doesn't know what he does—she insisted on taking their father's signet ring—the clan seal.

Some day she will realise that he's doing this for them both. France might be hide bound by the *Ancien Regime*, but is Britain any better? He knows of seats at Westminster where there's only a handful of voters—the landowner and his people. King George has been hidden from sight this past year, and there's talk of madness.

Johnny hasn't been idle. He's helped Marat with his writing, and le Maitre has kept him busy, working on pamphlets. The Abbe Sieyes "*Qu'est-ce que le Tiers État?*" *What is the Third Estate?* has identified it as the nation of France. Marat's response, *Offering to the Nation* has built up the need for the people to have a voice. Everyone with an interest in change has been scribbling over the past year. Even the Assembly of Notables who insisted on calling the Estates General have known that change needs to come. So far, the members elected are from the wealthy bourgeoisie: landowners, lawyers and bankers.

From that letter he read this evening, he's found useful intelligence. If Jacob Rose has a place in the Third Estate, then his sister, as the man's clerk, can report back to him.

He watches as the sedan chair is carried to the gate and Jacob alights, paying the chair men and bidding them goodnight. He sees him go into the house and the glow of his candle is dimly visible through the shutters. He looks up to the window of Jeannie's attic. Has he been cruel? Like him, his sister is hungry—in her case for knowledge and learning. She'd have been wasted as a servant companion to an old lady. He tells himself he's done her a favour. Jean the clerk has employment—an apprenticeship that can lead to a good living—but only if she can keep up the pretence.

He hoped he sounded convincing about the innkeeper's daughter. He's rather enjoyed flirting with the empty-headed little fool, but his interest in her is for another reason, one that he's yet to tell Marat about.

The light vanishes, reappearing in Jacob's window on the first floor.

Johnny slinks off into the darkness, darting through side streets and alleys until he reaches the back lanes where Le Maitre is waiting for him.

The press is inked up, ready for tomorrow's pamphlets.

He nods to Johnny as he sheds his coat and waistcoat, rolling up the sleeves of his shirt. 'You're late.'

The Scottish Agent

'I've got news. I know someone who will be in the Assembly, and his clerk can be our spy.

Chapter Ten

May 4th, 1789

The journey to Versailles, fifteen miles from Paris, took most of the day. The coach, laden with others attending the first meeting of the Estates General as observers, was poorly sprung and Jacob is weary and his bones ache, by the time they pull into the town square. The little town is a confection of pretty market stalls and the sugared almond town houses of the nobility and courtiers, most of whom spend their days and nights at the palace but require establishments of their own.

Geddes has arranged for him to stay in Francine's sister's family house in the town, and he is greeted by a footman in full livery, who shows him into the library where Francine is sitting with her sister, Henriette. For now, he has left Jean behind, in charge of catching up with the routine work. The lad has had enough experience now to draft a Will or deal with a transfer of deeds. He can trust him with the house and the petty cash.

Jacob has managed to avoid becoming a member of the

Assembly. Instead, as a compromise, he is to attend as an observer. There's a letter of recommendation signed by two of the 600 Third Estate deputes, which Geddes used his connections to obtain. He still feels uneasy.

He has tried to ask about Jean's sister, but the lad remains reticent, only saying that she is staying with a good family, and his wages will pay for her keep. He felt ashamed and handed the lad three gold pieces—an advance on his earnings. He's given him a holiday today—the lad is going to watch the grand procession from Notre Dame to the Place des Armes. The prospect of crowds appeals to the young, much more than it does to Jacob, who wants to be at Versailles a day early, to settle his thoughts.

Of greater concern is the innkeeper. Jules and his wife lost their tenancy and returned to service. Jacob wrote a reference for them, and he knows they are coachman and cook to Mercier's older brother, who has a thriving business in the town of Versailles. He has promised to try and seek out Lucette, to let her know where they now live, but without help from Francine and Henriette, that is a daunting task. Once she departed, Lucette appears to have vanished into thin air.

Henriette is fair, fat and forty, with powdered hair worn *a la mode,* and dressed in the latest court fashion. Her husband has a place at court, but she prefers to stay at their house. 'I hate the palace. Unless you have no sense of smell, it stinks of stale perfume that covers up sweat and bad breath.'

The *Roi Soleil* whose creation the palace was, did not include sufficient privies for the ten thousand courtiers and staff, and rather than walk the mile of corridors to the cess pit, servants discard the contents of chamber pots out of the nearest window.

'Besides, these days one hardly sets eyes on the Queen. She's too busy playing at being a shepherdess at her *petite*

Hameau.' There's a bitchy note to Henriette's voice.

There are in fact several palaces at Versailles. Besides the vast edifice that houses the Hall of Mirrors and overlooks the man-made lakes that cost so many lives, there is the Grand Commune, where the servants from the laundrymaids to Necker himself are housed, and both Grande and Petite Trianon. Marie Antoinette, sickened by the gossip and rumour of the affair of the Diamond Necklace, these days spends her days at Petite Trianon, with her closest circle, and the little farm is a place where she can relax. The Queen's House at the Hameau is light and airy, and much more comfortable than the palace.

The perpetrator of the scandal, the countess de la Motte was sentenced to be flogged and branded and thrown into the Salpetriere prison for life, but escaped to England, where she's been writing scandalous memoirs that hurt the Queen even more and are lapped up by her enemies. La Motte's poor dupe, Cardinal Rohan, lost everything and lives, a broken man, stripped of all titles, in an abbey in Auvergne. And the necklace? The jewellers Boehmer and Bassange who made it, intending to sell it to the old King Louis for Madam du Barry for 1,600,000 *livres*, lost everything. Geddes, hearing it had been broken up and sold in London, obtained several diamonds from it for Henriette.

Jacob looks pointedly at the diamond and pearl earrings she is wearing. She doesn't even bother to blush. He may dislike his hostess, but he is glad of room and board for the duration of the assembly, so he holds his tongue.

Henriette offers tea, and he enjoys the calming ritual as she takes the key from the silver chatelaine at her waist and unlocks a rosewood tea caddy, spooning the leaves into a silver pot. Tea is a luxury. The British control the sea lanes between Europe and China, and since the American Revolution, they've kept the French and Americans short of the precious stuff. That's why Cargill is welcomed at the Geddes house—his trade is not entirely legal. Jacob wonders, too, how young Etienne is settling into his new life.

She offers him a Sevres cup, exquisitely decorated with azure blue and gilded flowers. It's finer than the one in his home, and the small spoon in the saucer is silver gilt. He accepts a biscuit and sits on a spindly legged chair that he doubts can hold his weight.

Henriette's husband, recently ennobled, of course, is one of the 300 members of the Second Estate, participating in today's procession, while her uncle, an Archbishop is one of the First Estate. She mentions this *en passante* as they make polite conversation and he is aware that for her, the assembly has a different purpose.

Francine has the good grace to try to change the subject. She has been reading Mary Wollstonecraft's novel, and wonders what Jacob thinks of women turning their hand to fiction? Jacob tells her he enjoyed the book very much, and that he would encourage women to write, if they stick to fiction and do not indulge in scurrilous memoirs like La Motte. He applauds Wollstonecraft, an Irish governess, for taking inspiration from Jean Jacques Rousseau and making her heroine a resilient soul.

Ah, the joys of polite conversation—something which, as a bachelor, without women in his household, he endures only rarely. It is a relief when the ladies retire to their solar to work on their needlepoint, and he can spend an hour looking at the books on the shelves.

He pulls out a copy of Rousseau's The Social Contract, noting that the Swiss philosopher's works, along with those of Diderot, occupy an entire shelf. His host has a well-stocked library and while some of the books have uncut pages, there's signs he has been reading up on political theory. Should he take this as a positive sign? It's known that some of the nobles in the Second Estate would dearly like to curtail the powers of the King.

The footman is at the door, ready to show him to his room. Dinner is at nine o clock, when the master of the house returns, and he decides to take The Social Contract to while away the hours. Tomorrow will be exhausting.

Chapter Eleven

Jean accompanies Jacob as far as the departure point of the coach, watching him hoist his valise to the roof to be stowed with the other luggage. At the end of April, he asked about Jean's sister, and she answered as honestly as she could: Jeannie is living with good people who take great care of her, and Jean's wages will pay for her keep. He handed her three livres, and said they were for her sister, and would not affect her pay in September. She's had to find a safe place for her money—somewhere that Johnny won't think to look, if he sneaks in.

The crowds lined up to watch the procession are teeming with cut purses, and she's glad she didn't take anything of value with her. People are so desperate for bread; they will do anything to have the means to buy it—or steal it. The poor innkeeper and his wife were turned out of the inn, and there's no new tenant, so while Jacob is at Versailles, Jean's diet has been limited to what she can find in the markets and cook over the scullery fire. She's been living on porridge and oatcakes with broth, if she can find the makings at the market. With Jacob away at Versailles, she only needs to provide for herself. She is grateful for the housekeeping lessons she had at the Reverend's house in Aberdeen. His cook could do much with very little.

She crosses the road to stand beside Mercier, who has secured an excellent viewpoint outside Notre Dame. Of course, he's done well from this event. The procession numbers 1200 men, and half of those, the Third Estate, wear black overcoats with gold braid. He's been one of those supplying the braid. She compliments him on his business, but he still manages to look glum. 'I only profit if those men pay their accounts,' he grumbles.

The Third Estate men all carry candles, unless they are holding the ornate banners or are one of the King's Falconers.

It's a grand sight and it lifts her spirits—until she spots her twin a hundred yards away with Marat and Le Maitre. They appear to be trying to spot someone in the procession—someone they know among the deputies. She hopes they won't cause trouble.

The King, in a coat of gold, has a large diamond in his hat, in lieu of the crown, and is surrounded by his most senior Officers. The Queen is wearing a gown of cloth of silver and cloth of gold. She looks beautiful but troubled. There are cheers for her husband, but none for her. In the crowd, Jean hears the words *'Madame Deficit'* muttered. No doubt Johnny and Le Maitre have been at work with their pamphlets.

The procession moves onwards, through the Places des Armes to the Church of St Louis. Monseigneur de La Fare, the Bishop of Nancy is to give the address. Jean is swept along in the crowd and loses sight of Mercier.

She reaches St Louis, and while she doesn't manage to gain entry to the church, she joins a group outside an open side door, where she can just about hear the bishop speak.

He's blaming France's current difficulties on the extravagances of the Court. Jean is half shocked when there is loud applause—the first time that has ever happened in church. The King looks resigned, and his eyes are downcast. The Queen looks as if she has been turned to marble, stony faced and grim.

Jean turns and finds her brother grinning in triumph. He doesn't share her unease.

'Not off to Versailles yet, Johnny?' she hisses.

'Tonight,' he whispers. 'Just Le Maitre and me—we're going to walk all the way. Marat is getting a lift from a friend who's in there. I'm surprised you're not shuffling two paces behind Jacob. Why hasn't he taken you with him? Surely, he needs his clerk?'

She shakes her head. 'Not yet. He'll send for me when he does. I've got work to do in Paris.'

'Just wait, sister dearest. Great things are happening. That procession? That's the last gasp of the *Ancien Regime.*'

At a signal from Le Maitre, he's off, not even bothering to ask her to join him for food. She disentangles herself from the crowd, and only when she reaches home and retrieves the heavy key from its new hiding place, does she realise that her brass sleeve buttons have been cut off, and the small change removed from her pocket.

She removes her coat, sitting in shirt sleeves and waistcoat, and fills the kettle. Jacob has locked up the tea, but there's a bag of coffee beans that Cargill delivered and she's roasted enough of them to last a week. She uses the grinder and makes the strong drink. There's no milk, and she drinks it black, from a stoneware cup at her desk.

For some reason, she cannot get Marie Antoinette's face out of her mind. Anyone would have thought the poor woman was on her way to her execution. She shudders and lifts the quill.

CHAPTER TWELVE

Versailles, May 5th, 1789

The last time the Estates General met was in 1614, when Versailles was a mere hunting box, and the Court resided at the Louvre. The building that houses today's event is a temporary structure, with faux marble columns, built behind the Menus Plaisir building on the Avenue de Paris. Jacob can smell the fresh paint. It isn't actually a very large hall—it can barely accommodate the twelve hundred members and he's squashed in at the back, beside a portly bewigged man from the British Embassy who reeks of the peppermint lozenges he is taking from his waistcoat pocket.

The King and Queen are at the end of the hall, with the princes of the blood beside them. None of the royal party looks comfortable. The Embassy chap tells Jacob: 'That bishop at St Louis yesterday told them off roundly for extravagance—no wonder the Queen looks close to tears.'

Jacon nods, but there's talk also that the Dauphin's health is very poor, and the Queen was reluctant to leave his side.

The Scottish Agent

The deputies are sitting in rows around the edge of the hall. Jacob knows they have come from all corners of France and some of them have never even set food in Paris before, let alone Versailles. He's aware there are some members of the lower clergy and a few of the more politically minded nobles who are less than comfortable sitting with the First and Second Estate. Some, like the political theorist Abbe Sieyes and Comte Mirabeau have been elected to the Third Estate. Jacob scans the rows to try to spot the men that he knows, and sets eyes on his host, who is taking snuff from a tiny, enamelled box and sneezing delicately into a lace edged sleeve.

On the Third Estate bench a youngish looking man with immaculately powdered hair and a dandyish coat and knee breeches sits beside a large man with coarse features. They are deep in conversation but look up when the King begins the opening address.

Louis—the sixteenth of that name—sets out the circumstances that led to this convocation and tells the gathering what he expects from the Estates General. He calls himself a peaceful king and tells them that he is, indeed, the people's greatest friend.

Jacob thinks of the previous kings—from the Roi Soleil to the fifteenth Louis—who built up Versailles to imprison the nobles in a world of privilege and etiquette and cannot imagine either of them as the friend of ordinary French people. Both were far too remote. The man in front of him, it is said, likes to mend clocks and locks. In England, the king is called Farmer George. Is it better to have such men on thrones, or were they better off with those calculating despots?

Barentin, the Keeper of the Seals is speaking, and then, as Necker gets to his feet, the real business of the Three Estates begins. Jacob must commit this speech to memory.

Tonight, he will need to begin his reports on the day's proceedings.

Jacob has been introduced to Necker and knows him to be a man of principle—and a very able banker. The Swiss Calvinist knows the extent of France's economic calamity. He sets out the problem in simple language. The budget deficit is fifty-six million *livres,* and the purpose of this meeting is to agree on new taxation to cover it. The Third Estate are very unhappy. They are already collapsing under the weight of the taxes they pay. To let the Church and Nobles off lightly will no longer do. Jacob hears the whispers escalate to grumbling. Beside him, his companion offers a peppermint lozenge which he accepts. They won't be the only ones who will find this truth hard to digest.

Chapter Thirteen

Whatever Lucette imagined life at Versailles would be like, it certainly wasn't this. Her back aches from scrubbing the floor of the byre at *Le Petite Hameau*. Unlike most farms, this one is dainty and whitewashed, and every speck of dirt shows. Her frock—still the one she arrived with, is enveloped in a voluminous apron and her hair is covered with a mob cap, the frill of which gets in her eyes, because she has no time to starch it. These things would be noticed by the Queen, but her Majesty is at the hall where the Three Estates are meeting, and the major domo set the workers of Le Hameau to cleaning. The place must be immaculate for Marie Antoinette, the moment she can escape from her duties. It is her refuge and must be always ready.

The dainty little white goat that the ladies usually lead round with a pink ribbon has just spoiled Lucette's work by defecating on the floor she has spent the past hour scrubbing. Not for the first time, Lucette thinks longingly of home and Maman. Nobody has told her that home as she remembered it no longer exists. She has no idea that her parents are living less than three miles away in the town of

Versailles.

Home now is a box bed above the dairy at the Marlborough Tower, her few belongings stowed under her thin mattress, in an attic she shares with the head dairymaid, Avril, who snores loudly and keeps Lucette awake. They take their meals with the dairyman and his family—a serious man who says grace over even a cup of milk. She should not complain—food here is plentiful and of good quality, and she is well treated.

That night, less than a month ago, when she felt in her pocket for the coins the woman handed her, she found a piece of paper—a letter which directed her to apply to Monsieur Le Carre, if she wanted the opportunity to live and work at Versailles. She sneaked out that evening to go and visit her friend, Marie.

'Who is Monsieur Le Carre?' She showed her friend the letter.

Marie shook her head, 'I've never spoken to him, but the others say he chooses the servants who are placed with the most important nobles. Perhaps you might be a femme de chambre? Just think of the clothes you'd get?'

Lucette's feet hardly touched the cobbles as she dashed home to the inn. She packed her worldly goods—small as they were—into a valise that a customer left behind in lieu of payment. She folded her spare chemise and petticoat, added her ribbons and her slippers, her darned stockings and brushed her old cloak free of dust. She waited until her parents were at the door of their room to break her news.

To her dismay, her mother burst into tears and her father looked utterly downcast. 'You make a decision like this without telling us?' her mother sobbed.

Lucette half expected Papa to make a fuss and put his foot down—but he said little. She'd heard him speak downstairs of how hard times were, and his sad resignation broke her heart. She found sleep all but impossible, and at dawn, when she ate her meagre breakfast, red eyed and pale, she would have willingly changed her mind. Instead, Papa Jules walked with her to the square where the Versailles conveyance picked up Marie and herself. She hugged him and he kissed her cheek. His face was wet with tears. He whispered, 'Write to us, to let us know you are safe and happy.'

The two girls had seats at the back of the coach, and by the time they reached their destination, they were filthy from the dust of the road.

That first night she shared Marie's tiny cot, too exhausted to fight sleep, and she woke aching and miserable.

Versailles confused her—the King ate his meals in full view of an audience—he even went to bed with crowds watching and visited the commode with others in the room. When she asked Marie why, she used the word 'etiquette.' These were the rules set by Louis XIV who elevated himself to God like status. Lucette wondered if gods passed water in public? Even the servants had their own hierarchy, and when Lucette asked for Monsieur le Carre and showed her paper—which by now was crumpled, most of Marie's fellow laundrymaids looked blank. A footman visiting the laundry with an item from a duke squinted at it, noted the signature at the bottom, and commanded Lucette to follow him.

Monsieur le Carre, a short man, corseted into his satin frock coat, bewigged and rouged, barely looked up as Lucette curtsied deeply. She supposed that one would bow to the senior servants, but he waved a lace edged wrist at her and directed her to stand by the window, where he could look at her. She handed over her scrap of paper and he glanced at it, nodding when he saw the signature.

'Madame Gregoire sent you? Good, good. Tell me, girl, have you ever milked a cow or a goat?'

The unexpected nature of the question caught her unawares. 'Yes, Monsieur, at my uncle's farm.'

He pulled paper from a drawer of the spindly legged desk and dipping a goose feather quill in an exquisite porcelain inkwell, he scribbled several sentences in a spidery scrawl. He blotted the paper, folded it twice and sealed it, using a stamp with the seal of his office. He pulled the bell chord and summoned a footman. 'Gather your belongings and Georges here will escort you to Le Hameau.'

'Monsieur,' she breathed. Le Hameau meant she must be working for the Queen.

Georges, she found, was inclined to talk to her. She returned to pack her little bag, and met him at the door, where he waited with a pony and trap. He stowed her bag and offered a hand to help her climb onto the seat beside him. He took up the reins, clicked his tongue and the grey pony trotted sprightly on the path to Trianon.

He was curious. 'How do you come to have a letter of recommendation to Monsieur le Carre, if you've never been to Versailles before?'

She told him about Madame Gregoire's visit to the inn, and he frowned. 'All I can say is that it is very unusual for Madame to do favours for anyone, unless she expects something in return. Who did you say your parents are?'

The names, he said, were unfamiliar, so he asked where she came from.

'Paris,' she answered, simply. After all, she had lived nowhere else, and if he wanted to know where her parents came from, it was from an estate near Combs la Ville where her father had been a footman and her mother a cook.

'What work shall I be doing at le Hameau?' she asked. 'Will I be a maid to Her Majesty?'

He grinned. 'What did Monsieur le Carre ask if you could do? None of the palace servants are allowed near the

Queen's little farm. She suspects us of spying on her. Only new girls, untouched by our decadence will do as her farm workers. Perhaps that's what Madam Gregoire has in mind for you? You might be her little spy, reporting to her about what the Queen does and says?

She glanced shyly at Georges. He wore his livery well, and under his court wig, there were traces of fair hair visible. The court servants, she realised were all playing a part, in elaborate stage costume. If they were all like Le Carre or Georges—she wasn't quite so sure she wanted to be here.

Now, as she cleans the floor yet again, and looks sadly at the ruin of her only gown, she wonders if being married to a man like Mercier would be so bad after all?

She thinks of Le Maitre's apprentice, the lad who winked at her and touched her hand when she poured his wine. Will she ever see him again?

Chapter Fourteen

May 10th, 1789

Jacob's head hurts. He has escaped to his lodgings to write his account of the day's proceedings. Every day is the same. Nothing but talk and argument, not about dealing with the deficit—but about the nature of the meeting, and the demand of the Third Estate for a vote for each member.

He feels sorry for Barentin, charged with the running of the meetings—but with his hands tied. Necker, after his first statement which laid out the sorry state of France's finances, has been holding back—waiting for stalemate, before actively taking any action.

His host has invited Mirabeau to a reception at his house. The Comte has argued valiantly to keep all three estates in the same room—much to the disgust of the Church, who want the meetings to take place separately. Mirabeau is entitled to sit with the Second Estate—but was elected to the Third—and it is his passionate wish that the representation question is resolved so they can move to deal with the deficit. The concern of the Nobles and clergy is that they will lose more to the six hundred members of the Third Estate than they would gain in power at the expense of the King

Jacob has but an hour before the guests arrive and he sits at a small desk in his room, writing notes in a leather-bound journal that is already half filled with his tidy script. He must buy another soon, and not for the first time wishes that he had Jean here to act as secretary and run errands.

Finishing his task, he strips off his coat and waistcoat, rolls up the sleeves of his shirt and washes his hands and face at the washstand. The soap, like everything else in this house, is scented with lavender. He changes his stock for a fresh one and gives his coat a quick brush before putting it on again. He checks his reflection in the gilded mirror, before closing the door behind him and descending to the grand hallway. Mirabeau and his host are deep in conversation, but Henriette takes his arm and guides him to a woman perching on a window seat.

There is something familiar about her, but Jacob cannot quite place her. When she speaks, it is in English. 'How are you enjoying Versailles, Jacob Rose?'

The use of his first name catches him unawares. 'Ah—you forget we were recently introduced by Monsieur Marat?'

Her dress is that of the court—a rich, dark blue silk, with a *fichu* trimmed with lace, and her hair is powdered. There is a silk patch on her right cheekbone and her cheeks are lightly rouged. The last time he saw her, she was wearing the dark serge of a bourgeois, and her hair was left its natural dark auburn. 'Mistress Gregory? How remiss of me.'

She taps him on the arm with her closed fan. 'I shall forgive you. And my name, as well you know is Suzanne.'

'What brings you to Versailles, Suzanne?' he asks, trying to fathom how such a *grande dame* was dining in a humble inn, with the likes of Marat.

'My husband is a deputy, but I have business at court. I

have a talent for bringing people together who might not otherwise meet. Of course, it helps my husband if I can be *au fait* with court gossip.'

'What is the subject of court gossip, might I ask?'

'The King is already worried that the deputies are trying to seize power. He might revert to type and close the meetings. It's in everyone's best interest to get reform done—otherwise the more radical—like Maximillien and Georges over there, might take matters into their own hands.'

'Friends of Marat?' he asks. Maximillien looks too prissy to be one of Marat's ink-stained associates; Georges Danton on the other hand he recognises from the inn.

'Let us just say that they are aware of one another. These times make strange bedfellows, don't you think? After all, you appeared to be rather friendly with Jean Paul, or am I mistaken?'

'We occasionally eat in the same inn, and he asks me of the news from Scotland. That does not, necessarily make us friends.'

He wonders why Henriette was so eager to bring them together. 'Is there something you wanted from me?'

She accepts a glass of wine from a passing flunkey and raises it to her lips. 'You asked our hostess about a girl who left Paris to be a servant at Versailles?'

He feels a stab of guilt. He hasn't thought about poor Jules for days now.

'The daughter of the innkeeper where we first met. She left in a hurry and while her father has written to find where she is, he has had no reply. He and his wife are living in the town here now, returned to being servants and they want Lucette to know of their whereabouts. Can you help?'

'I know the Comptrollers—I would be happy to make enquiries for them. I shall let you know if I find the girl.'

The Scottish Agent

Jacob thanks her and looks around the room. Mirabeau is deep in conversation with Maximillien—who he understands is a lawyer like himself, but from Arras, and an elected deputy. His host is holding forth with a group of richly dressed men, one of whom looks very unwell, although under court dress and powdered wig, anyone would look pale. Jacob doesn't hear much of the conversation, but the group are upset about something.

It's a mild evening, and Jacob finds it hard to breathe in the crowded room. He nods to the footman at the door and tells him he is going out to take the air. He walks down the Avenue de Paris and turns off at a side street into a square, where the merchants who supply the needs of the court live. He finds the close leading to the stables of Mercier's brother's establishment and greets Jules, who is sweeping the old straw. He bids him good evening and tells him of his conversation with Suzanne Gregory. 'She has connections at Court—if anyone can help you find Lucette, she can.'

Jules, he can see has aged a decade in the space of a month. There is grey at his temples that wasn't there before and the lines on his face have deepened. 'Lucette showed me the letter of introduction—it was signed by a Madame Gregoire.'

This is news to Jacob—but he assures Jules this is a coincidence. He walks swiftly back to the house, but when he looks for Suzanne—she has already gone.

Chapter Fifteen

May 29th, 1789

Mirabeau has tried to keep the entire Assembly meeting in one hall and communicating with one another. He hasn't succeeded and while the Third Estate remain in the Hall, if Jacob wants to hear what is going on with the Nobles or the Clergy, he either needs to go to the other halls, or to meet with their members outside.

He is on his way to rendezvous with a clergyman member of the First Estate, when he sees Jean. He is torn between delight at seeing his clerk, and annoyance that he has left the office unattended, but approaches him anyway. 'Jean? What's the matter? Why didn't you send word you were coming?'

The young man doffs his hat, in acknowledgement, but looks blank. 'I fear you have mistaken me for someone else?'

Jacob realises his mistake—the young man has a more pronounced Adam's apple than Jean, and his features are harder, but there is a strong resemblance. They nod to one another and walk in opposite directions.

The Scottish Agent

Johnny has an assignation, and he passes the grandest of the noble's houses, walking into a quiet street, where some of the deputies have rented rooms. He congratulates himself on deceiving Jacob—but it was a close call, and he doesn't want to do anything that can spoil his little arrangement with his sister. The last thing he needs is to have Jeannie exposed and thrown back to live under his care.

The door is unlocked, by prior arrangement. Silently, and walking on tiptoe, he mounts the stairs and taps three times on the first door on the left. It opens, and she is there, naked under her silk wrap, which falls open as she takes his hand and draws him into the room. He shoves the door shut and pulls her into his arms.

'Did anyone see you?' she asks, taking his face in her hands and kissing him, first with closed mouth and then opening his lips with her tongue.

When the kiss ends, he shakes his head. 'I saw the Scotsman—Rose—I think he thought I was someone else.' He hasn't shared his secrets with her, and he knows she guards her own fiercely.

'Where's your husband?' he asks, stripping off his coat and jacket, looking furtively around the room. It's a pretty room, with a four-poster bed and hand painted wallpaper in the Chinese fashion. The covers are drawn aside, invitingly and she's closed the shutters to prying eyes.

'He's at the meeting, and afterwards he will dine with friends. They have business this evening.' He must look scared because she continues, 'Don't worry—I don't expect him back before midnight. Plenty of time for you to pay attention to more pressing matters.' She lets the robe drop to the floor, and presses her body against him, kissing his neck as she unwinds his stock and pulls his shirt over his head.

Her figure is perhaps a tad fuller than girls of his own

age, but he likes that, and the fact that she has more experience. They've only known each other a few months, but in that time, she has taught her young lover how to please her. He hasn't told her his real name—he is known to her as Jacques—but that also seems to excite her.

Le Maitre pushed him into her arms, telling him to tidy himself up and to try and gain entry to some of the salons—where an ability to quote Voltaire and Rousseau, and to discourse on the news from America can open doors. There appears to be few doors that are closed to Madame Gregory—and she is known to enjoy gossip.

Now, she pours a glass of wine, sips from it and offers the glass to him. Setting it down, she walks to the bed and beckons him to join her. He pulls off breeches and stockings, and slides in beside her. He is hard and she takes him in her hand, smiling. 'Well, Jacques, it looks as if you are pleased to see me.'

Suzanne Gregory—or Madame Gregoire—at thirty-five, is almost twice the age of Johnny Rose. Her husband will indeed be dining with Robespierre and Danton, but after dinner, he will be in the bed of his lover. She won't grudge him—she has trained Jacques to be the perfect bedfellow and she is going to enjoy the hours ahead. She knows perfectly well that Le Maitre—rogue that he is, has sent Jacques to spy on her, and she lets him have morsels that she wants the pamphleteers to use.

She is a woman in her prime, well fed, and gives the appearance of never having done a hard day's work in her life. Johnny knows he must pump her for information. She is the wife of a well-connected deputy, but he is not fully aware of her agenda. She purrs under him, as he takes her with the energy that only a nineteen-year-old can. She will need to work on his finesse, but he shows promise.

Later, as the sun sinks and the light outside turns to rose, she wakes him from the slumber that follows satisfaction. She pours another glass and says, 'What's Le Maitre printing this week?'

He takes the glass and drains it, and tries to pull her back into the bed, but she resists, laughing.

'We're leading on the problems the Nobles are causing— about the business of the Assembly.'

'What about the price of bread?'

'Eh?'

'Jacques,' she sighs, 'the bourgeoisie can always have food on their tables. My husband and the men in that hall don't know hunger, or how mothers feel when their children are starved. Change will no doubt start in the meeting halls, but the people of Paris need to feel that you understand them, and boring comment about votes is less important to them than the cost of a loaf.'

He's listening now. She presses her advantage home. 'Let us suppose that the Queen has made a tactless remark about the price of food, wouldn't that make them riot?'

'I suppose so,' he doesn't sound convinced.

'I've got a girl planted in the Queen's household,' Suzanne says. 'I can arrange for you to meet with her.'

It's time for a visit to young Lucette, she thinks. The girl's been on that little farm for weeks, and a present of a dress and some ribbons will be more than welcome. She can arrange a meeting with a familiar face from home. No doubt the young man in her bed will be able to use his newly acquired skills to wheedle information. She wants to know what the Queen does and says when she visits the little farm. She has other reasons for wanting Marie Antoinette to set eyes on this girl. It will be a shame to pass Jacques on to another woman, but if it helps her achieve her purpose, it will be a sacrifice well worth making.

Chapter Sixteen

June 14, 1789

Jeannie enjoys having the house to herself. By day she must work as usual, meeting Jacob's clients, and drafting documents, some of which she needs to send to Versailles for him to counter sign. It is the day-to-day work of a notary. The tenancy of a house; the Will of a widow; a grievance between neighbours.

She leaves the house early each morning to buy food, and she's noticing that her *sous* buy less and less. Today's loaf is small and poor quality, and the small cheese she haggled over is mouldy. The June heat makes food go off quickly unless it is stored in the cool and dark of the press in the cellar. She is at her desk before nine and she works through the daylight hours, eating her bread and cheese as she writes in her ledgers. Jacob is preoccupied with his work at Versailles, and she is doing his work as well as her own. Despite what she might have said to her brother, she enjoys the work.

The sun sets late, these hot summer evenings, but she has locked the front door and closed the shutters, and down in the cellar, she pulls out the copper tub the laundress uses for their washing and heated water to fill it a third of the way up. It's too small for most bathers, but if she sits in it, with her legs over the side, she can just about manage. She's lined it with an old sheet from the press, to stop the heat burning her back, and now she slips off her dressing robe, and lowers her body into the warmth with a deep sigh. Over this past month she has become used to this little luxury, and every week that Jacob writes to say he will not be home yet, is a relief for her. It means evenings when she can lose the restrictive corset and breathe properly.

She's become bold about opening the mail that is sent for Jacob. He's given Jean the clerk the authority to do so, but she's also read his private correspondence. Some of it, missives from Scotland, give her insight into Jacob's interests, which are more philosophical than political. A letter arrived this morning from the Reverend, asking after Johnny and his sister. It assumes that she has been living with Georgina Danby—news has yet to reach Scotland of the widow's demise. If Jacob sees this, he might press her about Jeannie's whereabouts, and she can't keep fobbing him off.

She draws the rough washcloth over her arms and scrubs at a patch of dry skin on her elbow. She needs some salve for it, but as a boy, she must tell the pharmacy that it is for a sister, or an employer. Besides, the petty cash box is almost empty. If Jacob isn't coming home, she will need to send out invoices and gather up payment.

Would she want to return to being Jeannie? She would need to find work as a companion or governess—she has no marriage portion, and little chance of finding a husband. She passes quite well as a young man, where she isn't judged by her looks. Mousy hair, slightly protuberant eyes and a terror of childbirth do not appeal to most men seeking a wife. Living under the roof of her current employer, with access to his books, and working and studying the law texts as his apprentice, she is adding to her education. Who knows, if she can maintain the pretence, she might even become a notary in her own right.

She rises from the bath and dries herself, before drawing her nightshirt over her head, and pulling on the threadbare dressing gown. She will need to tidy the bath water away, throwing the pail over the cobbles of the yard, once it is too dark for passers-by to see her.

On the desk by the window is a pamphlet. There is no need to ask who has written it. Johnny and Le Maitre are getting bolder. She can only hope that he doesn't spoil this for her, the way that he spoils everything else.

Chapter Seventeen

June 18th, 1789

Jacob wants his own home and his own bed. He would dearly like to return to his day-to-day work and his routine. He is thoroughly sick and tired of French politics. Most of all, he is weary of Henriette and the round of receptions and dinners that mean he must put up with disgruntled nobles, and churchmen, and even worse, fellow lawyers who are getting a taste for all of this.

The Third Estate call themselves the Communes or Commons now. 'After all, that is what your English parliament calls itself?' the Abbe Sieyes remarks over dinner. He doesn't notice Jacob flinch. The Act of Union of 1707 meant it is not the English but the British parliament these days. He tries to correct the Abbe, but he has turned to the man on his other side and is conversing about the quality of the wine.

The Communes have all but given up on the Church and the Nobles, and flushed with their determination for change, have declared themselves to be an Assembly and their intention is to draft political reform without them, if necessary. They have rejected the old ways of having one vote for each of the three groups, where they could be outvoted by them. Instead, with one vote per assembly member, they know they can outvote the Church and aristocracy. There are rumours the King bitterly regrets ever allowing them to meet at all, now. Who knows when he will decide to put a stop to it?

Louis XV said, 'Apres moi, le deluge.' Did he know the mess that his grandson would make of being king?

Jacob's notebook is filled now. He spends his days in the stuffy hall, committing every word to memory, and transcribes his observations in the hours before dinner at his host's table. After dinner, his work becomes more serious, as he writes letters to his masters in Scotland. The most delicate require ciphers, and he burns the originals in his fireplace, until they blacken and turn to ash that no curious servant can read.

Three days later, his worst fears are realised. The King, backed up by his privy council decides enough is enough. He gives orders to close the hall where the National Assembly meets. He wants the three estates to meet separately and an end to the one member one vote nonsense.

The Assembly turns up to find themselves locked out, with Royal guards blocking their way and they cast around for a space large enough to hold the Commons, and those clergy who have thrown their lot in with them. Jacob sees that lad he mistook for his clerk hovering on the edge of the group, along with Jean Ignace Guillotin, and Jean Sylvain Bailly yelling 'To the Tennis Court!' Off they troop. The covered real tennis court is not ideal, but it offers space large enough for the gathering. What happens in the coming hours will change everything.

There is much excitement over what has happened, and

fear that they might be divided and arrested. They take a solemn vow—never to separate and to reassemble and continue to meet until they have settled the constitution of France.

Jacob wonders if this might be a good time to absent himself and return to Paris and his office and to escape this burden, but he's known to many of the deputies by now, and they decide they need officers for their Assembly. These will not be diplomats or deputies—but the observers are not exempt. By the time all the three groups meet, he has become an Usher.

In his room he puts his head in his hands and sighs. He is caught between hammer and anvil. In his life he has never sought out attention—he might read of political change—but to be part of it may come at a cost he is neither willing nor able to pay. He writes to his masters in Scotland to explain that this prevents his reporting to them. As an Usher, he is employed by the Assembly, which expects and commands his loyalty. Sandy Geddes, dining with his wife's family brings the response: he is to continue to make his reports. There is no escape. He must proceed with caution.

Chapter Eighteen

June 30th, 1789

Lucette feeds the fluffy chickens and gathers in the eggs on the tiny farm. She milks the goats and the cows and scrubs out the dairy. Sometimes, Avril lets her help to make the butter, and to separate the cream. She carries out her duties willingly, but at the Hameau's small farm the servants might as well be on a desert island, for all they see of the court, or indeed any of the army of staff at Petite Trianon, let alone the palaces of Versailles. Yes, the Queen comes to the Hameau, but often she does not visit the farm. Instead, she arrives, settles herself at the Queen's house, attended by a handful of servants whose loyalty is beyond doubt. The door is closed to anyone outside that circle.

Lucette might as well be invisible. She is expected to keep her head down, to do as she is told and to remain silent unless addressed directly.

It has been a dismal month. The young Dauphin, whose ailing health has been the cause of the Queen's misery, died, and the visits to the Queen's House have been subdued.

The Scottish Agent

When Lucette has taken her evening walk nearby—the only hour she has to herself in a day—she has heard sobbing. The little boy was only eight years old.

'Consumption,' Avril says, 'these last two years. At least he's with God now.' She crosses herself.

Tomorrow, however, Lucette has a treat: for the first time since she arrived at the Hameau, she has a morning off, and the farmer is taking her with him to the small market in the town of Versailles. There, she can look at the stalls, and perhaps use the small sum she is paid to buy a treat?

She has a letter for her parents. She hasn't dared to ask if she could send it before. In it, she has poured out her regret for her decision, and prays that they can forgive her.

The ride to the town gives Lucette the chance to look around her. Used to the bustle of Paris, and the peace and quiet of the Hameau, the town of Versailles is a compromise—pretty buildings, and plenty to look at. The cart passes by Mercier et Fils, where her mother is sweeping the bedroom floors and doesn't look out of the window to see Lucette. Neither does Jules, in his livery, opening the doors for customers, look twice at the girl. Of course, she does not look for them—as far as she knows they are at home in Paris.

The farmer draws the cart up and tells her where to post her letter. 'Be back here at noon. Any later and you'll need to walk.'

The market overwhelms Lucette's senses. The colours, scents and sounds are music to her ears, and she counts the few coins in her pocket and decides to look around, before she spends them. She longs for a new dress and finds her way to the stalls where second hand clothing is sold. Perhaps a petticoat or a new apron? A new set of laces? She asks the prices and backs away, in resignation.

Suzanne watches her with amusement. She walks several

paces behind the girl and has Lucette's letter in her pocket. She's followed Jacob on his visits to the former innkeeper and hidden in the shadows as the man poured out his woes. Years of being discreet to his former masters, and his distress at his eviction mean he's told Jacob details that confirmed her hopes.

She steps forward and touches the girl on her elbow. 'Lucette? You look well. How are you enjoying life at Court?'

Lucette looks blankly at her. Of course, Suzanne looks different from that night at the inn, with her fine clothes and powdered hair.

'You are mistaken, Madame. I am a dairymaid.' Lucette's voice has lost its vivacity, and her posture is subservient. Perhaps she has gone a tad too far in her plan? The girl before her is a farmhand, from the work roughened hands to the ugly sunburn on her arms and breast.

'Lucette!' Suzanne smiles as Jacques dashes across the square and kisses Lucette on both cheeks, before lifting her in his arms and swinging her round. The power of youth to reawaken the senses, she reflects. She signals to Jacques over the girl's head before she leaves the market. It is down to him now.

'Monsieur! It is so lovely to see a familiar face. I miss Paris so much! Is there news of my parents?' she asks.

He's rehearsed this. He knows perfectly well where Jules and his wife live now, but answers, 'I'm sorry, Lucette, but they left Paris only weeks after you came here. They left no forwarding address.'

Her shoulders droop and her eyes fill with tears. He steps closer and puts an arm under her before she sinks to the ground, like a hot air balloon that has deflated.

'I know someone who can help us find your mama and papa,' he says. 'But first, you look as if you could use a drop of wine to put some roses back in your cheeks.'

The Scottish Agent

He takes her hand and leads her past the stalls to where a vendor has sweet wine and delicate pastries for sale.

He feels sorry for the girl, but not so sorry that he will defy Suzanne's instructions. She has plans for Lucette, and he will need to use every bit of his charm to deliver the silly little girl who has no idea of how useful she will be to them.

Chapter Nineteen

The dress is perfect, Suzanne reflects. It should be—enough effort has gone into finding it. She bribed the bursar at the convent, to let her look through the garments surrendered by their novices. It's a simple girl's frock, twenty years out of fashion, but with a simplicity that makes it suitable for a dairymaid. Rose pink, with a striped petticoat in the English fashion, it was made for a girl of Lucette's age. It will fit perfectly, and it is only right that it should belong to Lucette. There are little rosebuds embroidered on the bodice. Anyone who knew the original wearer will recognise this garment. Suzanne is counting on this.

Jacques steers Lucette to a little shop in a back street, where he tells her he's seen something that is perfect for her. Inside, on tables, garments are laid out for inspection. She looks at grand court dresses that reek of stale perfumes and have stains on the bodices and wrinkles her nose. She hesitates at a dress of striped, blue cotton, fingering the fabric. Jacques draws in his breath, willing her to move on towards the pink. Instead, she turns away. 'Monsieur, I have not enough money. We must go.'

The Scottish Agent

'Look at the pink, Lucette. It's your colour.' Jacques takes her hand and leads her to the table where the dress is waiting. She draws in her breath, and smiles. 'It is pretty, but I cannot afford it. It is too fine for me.'

The old Lucette, the one from the inn, would have clapped her hands and danced in delight, but this one has tears in her eyes.

'Let me buy it for you,' he says, gently. 'When you see your parents again, you want them to see how pretty you are and how well you are doing? We'll get it wrapped for you, and you can try it on when you get home.'

Her shoulders droop. 'I have no looking glass.'

He calls for the shopkeeper. 'Is there a place where Mademoiselle can try this dress on?'

The shopkeeper—or rather Suzanne's maid, who has paid the shop's owner to take an early lunch—bustles her into a small room with a looking glass and unlaces her, until she is standing in her shift and stays, blushing. The skirt of the dress is held out for her to step into and then the bodice and sleeves are eased on to her body. The laces are pulled tight and fastened, and she can see her reflection in the glass.

Suzanne, standing in the shadows, breathes a sigh of relief. She was right. The dress could have been made for Lucette, and it is the perfect colour for her.

The clock chimes half past eleven. Lucette is alarmed. 'I must be back at the market! If I don't come in time, I must walk and I do not know the way.'

She is helped out of the dress and into her own garment and the lovely frock is folded carefully and placed into a drawstring calico bag. She takes Jacques' arm, and by the time she arrives at the cart, there is a hint of a smile on her face. The farmer is ready to go, and he clicks his tongue in frustration at her tardiness. Jacques hands her into the cart, and places her precious bag in her lap, before bowing to her, as if she really is a lady of quality.

The cart rumbles out of the square, and as it moves, Jacob, crossing the square, catches a glimpse of the girl on the seat beside the driver. Lucette looks happy enough. At least he can report that to Jules and tell him that she is well.

Chapter Twenty

July 11th, 1789

The Bastille is a bastion of the Old Regime. It stands firmly guarding the Porte Saint Antoine to the east of the city, and its eight massive towers have stood since the Hundred Years War, over four centuries proving impregnable to old enemies. The guards, standing on the battlements have an excellent view over the city, if they can be bothered to climb to the top.

These days it stores gunpowder, and houses but a handful of prisoners. One of these has driven his jailors mad, with his antics. The jailor tells Le Maitre, over a drink in a rough tavern of the Italian who sings all through the night and has written musical notation all over the walls of his cell with a sharp flint.

'Not as if we don't feed him and put up with his caterwauling,' the prison guard mutters, gulping his wine and tearing a chunk of a stale loaf to spread with cheese. 'We even let him out of the cell to walk in the yard, and he sings his bloody heart out.'

'What's his crime?' Le Maitre asks, pouring another drink into the guard's outstretched cup.

'Falling for the wrong girl,' he replies, 'but if you ask me his singing is bloody criminal.' He wipes his wet mouth on a grubby sleeve.

'Locking a man up for singing and falling in love sounds a bit extreme to me,' says Le Maitre's friend, Jacques.

The guard shovels more bread and cheese into his gob and chews vigorously, open mouthed. Jacques notices the man's blackened teeth and feels sick. Le Maitre nudges him, signalling *Keep him talking.*

'It's how they did things before this King took over. If a man annoyed a noble, they could get a *lettre de cachet* and put them away for good. In the old days of course, they'd throw them into an *oubliette* and forget about them. This Louis, of course, is too soft. Doesn't believe in doing away with prisoners on the quiet. That's why we need to put up with them. Any more of that cheese?' he shouts across to the bar keeper, who shakes his head.

'Who pays for their keep?' Le Maitre asks.

'You're writing one of those pamphlets?' the man asks, looking suspicious.

'Don't worry,' Jacques soothes him, 'We'll leave your name out of it.'

'If they've broken laws, then they're prisoners of the state. But if they've been, you know, put away, then the aristo who wanted them out of the way must stump up.'

'And that would be?'

'More than my job's worth,' he says, draining his cup, belching and standing up, drawing on his coat. 'Sorry, Monsieur—but that will cost you, and I'm going on guard now. They watch him move unsteadily towards the door and cross the cobbled street.

Le Maitre and Jacques exchange glances. Jacques digs in

his pockets for coins to pay for their drinks and they set off round the corner to the print shop.

Tonight's pamphlet is of vital importance. They came hotfoot from Versailles with the news that Necker has been sacked. The king's great hope has let him down, and there's talk that the Assembly itself is in danger.

Perhaps the Assembly went too far abolishing all taxes, intending to start again, Necker had suggested. He could go to them and steer them in the right direction, but Louis, fearing that his finance minister wanted France to be ruled as Britain was, with a constitutional monarchy, ordered him out. Artois and Marie Antoinette insisted that Necker left the country, in case he went behind the King's back.

Le Maitre observes, 'Necker's been sacked before. He'll be back.'

'What if he can't come back?' Jacques is setting the type for the pamphlet and doesn't look up. He misses the grim set of Le Maitre's jaw.

'Desmoulin's given us our orders. If Necker stays sacked, then it's civil war.'

It's a dangerous moment. There are thirty thousand troops in and around Paris, and not all of these are French. Louis and Marie Antoinette have requested help from her family, and the presence of foreign soldiers in Paris is making people uneasy. The Assembly requested their removal, but the King, for once is standing firm. The troops, he says are there to keep order. Marat and Le Maitre scoff at this, but they keep their bags packed, in case they need to leave in a hurry.

'What's your interest in those prisoners?' Jacques asks.

'I want to know if any of them are political prisoners. We need an excuse to get into the Bastille. I doubt anyone will lift a finger to help a musician.'

'To work, Jacques. We need these to hand out at the

Julie MP Adams

Palais Royale tomorrow.'

Chapter Twenty-One

July 12th, 1789

Jeannie, returning from a morning errand, and considering stopping for lunch, sees the crowds gathering outside the Palais Royale. She looks around the crowd, spotting her twin handing out his wretched bits of paper. She snatches one from a woman and scans it swiftly. It is the news of Necker's dismissal, and the mood on the street is angry.

She's had messages from Jacob, instructing her to keep herself safe but to write a record of any unrest she sees in the streets of the capital.

She's jostled into the heart of the crowd, with a workman's elbow digging in her chest. She bites her tongue to stop crying out in pain.

There are two waxworks from Curtius' workshop being held aloft. One of them is the image of Necker, the other the Duc D'Orleans, who is enjoying the limelight, as he places himself on the side of the Assembly, thumbing his nose at his cousin the King and his Queen.

Her twin and his friend Le Maitre must have had

knowledge of Necker yesterday—they've been busy, and the waxworks and the pamphlets indicate this is no sudden gathering.

Not every member of the crowd is angry at the King. A woman in fine clothing, who Jeannie has seen with Francine Geddes, is saying something. She cannot hear, but it has clearly annoyed other people nearby who are beating her and pulling at her hair. The hair is a powdered wig, and the woman's own tresses, wispy and lank are being tugged out in handfuls. Her clothing is already torn and there's blood at the corners of her mouth. She is a broken doll by the time they have finished with her. The viciousness of the attack makes Jeannie feel sick. Worse still, she doesn't dare offer any help, but must turn her back, lest they hurt her too.

The crowd has swelled. Where there were hundreds gathered in the gardens, Jeannie can hardly move now—there are thousands heading to the Café Foy. There, a man she has heard both her twin and Jacob talk of—Camille Desmoulins—has climbed onto a table and is addressing the crowd. She can see Le Maitre and her brother standing close to him, cheering him on.

She's heard this sort of talk back in Scotland. Johnny was arrested for speaking about politics down in the taverns on Aberdeen docks, but he had nothing on this man, who knows how to stir up the feelings of his listeners. If the crowd had not been already discontented and ready to march, his peroration reminding them that what happened to Necker could lead to another St Bartholomew's Eve Massacre, has them roaring their support. When he declaims, 'I would rather die than submit to servitude!' Jeannie feels her hair standing on end.

The crowd follow him to the Champs Elysse's where a German cavalry unit is waiting, armed and ready for them. She can hear the jingling of harness and smell the tension in the air.

Jeannie struggles to leave the mob. If she tries too hard, she will draw attention to herself. She tells her body to go limp, and as men in *sans culottes*—the loose trousers worn by workmen—march past her, she retreats to the edge of the angry sea.

Out of the corner of her eye, she sees the woman's bleeding body carried away. Forgetting her earlier hunger she makes her way home, feeling sick to her stomach at what she has witnessed.

She slumps down at Jacob's desk, drawing a sheet of paper and a quill to her, and sets out to write her account of what she saw.

The little house is a sanctuary, but despite locking the door and closing the shutters, she doesn't feel safe. The noise of the mob echoes in her head and she must wait until the next day to hear the outcome from the baker as he hands over her small loaf. His brother, he says, was with the mob as they pelted the soldiers with chairs and rocks. 'They retreated,' he says with satisfaction.

'The mob?'

'No,' he laughs, 'The soldiers. They're scared of us now. They charged at our citizens, and they didn't win.'

Chapter Twenty-Two

July 15th, 1789

Mirabeau calls on Jacob and his host, early. Jacob is eating breakfast. The morning room is bright, with sunshine dancing on the polished surface of the table. A gilded clock on the mantelpiece chimes the hour. The brioche roll on Jacob's fine china plate is half eaten and he asks the footman to set a place for his visitor, and to bring fresh coffee. The statesman and the usher have an unlikely friendship, but both are aware that the Assembly has changed everything. 'News from Paris,' he says. His hands are shaking. 'Our young friends have gone too far.'

The rioting that Jean witnessed continued for two days, with the crowd breaking into government buildings and seizing weapons before setting the buildings alight. Angry, hungry people broke into the Monastery of Saint Lazare and looted the food.

Thirty thousand muskets were taken from Les Invalides, but there was no ammunition for them. The mob headed for the Bastille where it is known gunpowder is stored.

The Scottish Agent

'There were a thousand of them, Monsieur Rose.'

'As few as that? The Bastille is impregnable, isn't it? The walls are eight feet thick, and there's a garrison, isn't there?'

'That garrison is where the old soldiers have an easy life. There are only about eighty of them, and a few Swiss guards. They were outnumbered ten to one.'

'Surely the cannons could be fired on the mob?'

The statesman shakes his head. 'Fire on the people? That would be a declaration of war, and even the King would not give that order. Besides, poor De Launey had no water and only enough food for a few days. He couldn't withstand a siege.'

'So, what happened then?'

'The delegates asked him to hand over the two hundred and fifty barrels of gunpowder and take down the cannon. He played for time and said he could do no such thing without direct orders from Versailles.

Jacob thinks of the Bastille as being like the Tower of London—impregnable. Mirabeau tells of how the mob cut the chains of the drawbridge and rushed into the courtyard. Shots were fired and later that day, mutinous veterans of the American War joined the mob.

'I gather it was carnage. De Launey tried to make terms, but the mob captured him and marched him to the Hotel de Ville.'

'Is he a hostage? Surely, they will treat him with respect?'

Mirabeau shakes his head. 'He's dead. The reports say that they beat him and kicked him all the way there and fell on him with sabres and bayonets. They hacked off his head with a knife and stuck it on a pike. When the mayor tried to protest, they killed him too.'

'And the mob? How many of them were killed?'

'Barely a hundred, my friend. If our own soldiers turn on us, then this is a terrible moment.'

'Do you regret the Assembly?'

Mirabeau shakes his head. 'We needed change, but I made the mistake of thinking that you British created the model for that change.'

Jacob drinks his coffee and wrinkles his face at its bitter taste. 'Our glorious Revolution came at the cost of a war: three wars, if you count the Pretenders. Wars that France financed.'

'That's what Rochefoucauld said to the King. Louis asked if the attack on the Bastille was a revolt. He told him, no, Sire, it is a Revolution.'

'What will the King do now?' Jacob asks.

'I spoke with him before I came here. He cannot leave the troops in Paris without risking all-out civil war. He will order them to leave the city.'

'Will he recall Necker?'

'Who knows? I think it is his only hope. He's going to make a speech later today. He's asking Lafayette to appear on the balcony with him, for support. He's terrified.'

Chapter Twenty-Three

The sound of hoofbeats clattering into the street goes unnoticed by the group of *sans culottes* who are celebrating the events of the previous day. The inn is rowdy and two revellers have already been thrown out for drinking beyond their means.

A slim figure, wrapped in a dark cloak, slips from the horse and tethers it outside a townhouse several doors from the inn. Three sharp swift knocks on the door are followed by two slow thumps. A bolt inside is drawn back and an arm reaches out to haul the newcomer inside.

Suzanne Gregory drops the cloak to show a trim figure in a dark wool riding habit. Her hair is unpowdered and shows its natural dark auburn. Her eyes glitter with excitement. 'Where is he?'

Jacques expected more of a greeting than this, but he puts her brusqueness down to the tumult of the last few days. He moves to kiss her, but she dismisses him with a gesture, and a frown. There are other men in the house and if she's recognised, one of them might tell her husband.

'Valenti? He's upstairs in the attics and he's not making

a lot of sense. Come up and see for yourself.'

The stairs of the house are a generous spiral, and they clatter up the stone treads, passing ornately carved wooden doors on the first and second floors, and plainer ones on the top landing.

The man in question is sitting on the edge of a cot bed, head in his hands. The room is lit by half a dozen candles and he finds the light too bright, after his dark cell. They've tidied him up a bit, Jacques explains to Suzanne. 'His hair was almost waist length and matted and he'd quite a beard, and his clothes were good quality but filthy.' They've dressed him in the manner of the mob, in *sans culottes*—loose linen trousers, shirt and a short jacket. His hair is shorn and he's clean shaven now.

She crosses to the man and takes his face in her hands, raising it so she can look into his eyes. At first, he twists his head to look away from her, but she persists, and he returns her gaze. There's a flicker of recognition as he tries to gather his thoughts.

'It's him. After all these years. Thankyou Jacques,' she says, and turns to go.

The man, who has said nothing, but has used music to communicate for almost two decades, speaks. His voice is slightly accented, and hoarse. 'Suzanne?'

She moves round to face him again. 'Gianfranco? You remember me?'

'Where is Ottilie? And what became of our child?'

Gianfranco Valenti is forty years of age. He was among the handful of prisoners freed by the mob from the Bastille, which has been his entire world for twenty miserable years. Placed there by *lettre de cachet* as punishment for marrying the daughter of a courtier without permission and fathering a child.

Those who hate Marie Antoinette speak of the retinue

she brought with her on her marriage—the Austrians and Italians who provided the music for her entertainments. After all, a young Mozart had played for her in Vienna, and she loved to be surrounded by music.

'I know where your daughter is. I will reunite you soon. Trust me,' Suzanne says.

'And Ottilie?'

'In the convent at Longchamps, as far as I know,' she replies. 'Her father is dying. Once he is dead, you can go there and claim her.'

Jacques thinks—but not before you have repaid us for getting you out of the Bastille.

Gianfranco Valenti has tears in his eyes, but these are tears of joy. He has waited a long time, and Suzanne assures him it will be a matter of days, rather than weeks until he can reclaim his bride and daughter.

Jacques and Suzanne descend the stairs. Le Maitre is waiting on the first floor and invites them into a book lined library. They take seats around an ornate table, where a decanter of brandy and a collection of glasses are placed. Le Maitre pours a glass and offers it to Suzanne who accepts. Jacques pours for himself. Le Maitre raises his glass and proposes a toast: 'To the Revolution!'

They clink glasses and drink. 'What do you have in mind for our guest upstairs?' asks Le Maitre.

Suzanne draws a paper from her bodice. 'This is the deposition of Jeanne de la Motte. It gives the history of the Queen's closest circle. Many years ago, I was at boarding school in Passy with Jeanne. Those of us without a fortune were destined for the nunnery at Longchamps. Another girl, two years older than us, Otillie de Saint Combs, was affianced to a Vicomte, and brought to Court to be one of the Queen's ladies.

'The Vicomte,' she continues, 'was twenty-five years

older than us, and a widower, with no children. He wanted a young and virtuous wife to give him sons and save his fortune and title from going to the nephew he detested. Moreover, he was the close friend of Otillie's father, who would benefit from the arrangement.

'Otillie was virtuous, and beautiful, and we detested her for her piousness. When she met her future husband and faced her duty, on the same day, Marie Antoinette arranged for her to take music lessons from Gianfranco Valenti—a musician of modest talent, but exceptional good looks. Even now, after many years locked up, he still has a look of the boy he was. Any other woman would have married the Vicomte but conducted a liaison with the music master. Otillie, however, had to marry where her heart dictated. The wedding took place in secret, in the chapel at Passy, with three of us as witnesses and when Otillie told her father, she was already carrying Gianfranco's child. She expected forgiveness. Instead, her father had the marriage annulled and threw her into the convent. The Vicomte issued a *lettre de cachet* and Gianfranco Valenti was imprisoned in the Bastille.'

'And the child?' Jacques asks.

'Given to servants to raise as their own. A twenty-year lease on an inn, belonging to the Vicomte. It took me years to find her, but I believe Lucette might yet make herself useful to the Revolution. I have a plan. I will use Valenti and his family to discredit Marie Antoinette.'

Chapter Twenty-Four

July 17th, 1789

'My dear, such excitement,' Henriette declares, sweeping into the library where Jacob is writing a report. Francine, sitting by the window with a book in her hand, sets the volume down and looks up at her sister.

'Come and see for yourself,' Henriette continues, taking her hand and drawing her out of the library to the salon at the front of the house. From the windows they can see a train of carriages, heavily laden with luggage moving swiftly along the road out of Versailles.

'They've decided to leave—Artois, Polignac, Conde—the men who called for Necker to go. I heard from Le Carre that they think war is likely and they are leaving to save their own necks. If anything happens to the King or his son, Artois is in line for the throne. He's off to Savoy, but I'd not be surprised if he goes to Austria.'

There's a smugness in Henriette's voice that Jacob finds repellent.

'Why aren't you in Paris with the Assembly to hear the

King?' she asks him.

'I have work here to complete,' he replies. 'The arrangements for the rest of the Assembly meetings this month. If the Assembly were to move to Paris, of course, I could return to my own house.' He has as little desire to remain under her roof as she has for him to be their guest.

'Besides, I know what is to happen. The King will appear on a balcony, wearing the new cockade, with Lafayette, and they will appoint Bailly as Mayor of Paris. That should please the crowds and when Necker returns, the Assembly can try to sort the financial affairs of the nation.'

He finishes the sentence he is writing, and says, 'Have you spoken with your friend Suzanne Gregory of late?'

There is a slight flush on Henriette's powdered face. 'The last I heard, she was going to Paris. Why?'

'She promised to help me look for a girl, who I have reason to believe is a servant in Versailles. The girl's parents are concerned for her,' he replies. He can tell she is lying, and he wonders why.

Henriette flounces out of the room, with a flick of her fan. Francine, who has returned to the window seat, says, 'Poor Jacob. You really don't like Versailles, do you?'

He sets his quill down and eases his back. 'I have my duties, but I would much sooner sleep in my own, hard bed and be beholden to no one.'

He pauses, and says, 'How well does your sister know Madame Gregory?'

Francine draws her pretty brows together in a frown. 'Their husbands are friends, but they knew one another at Passy—where we all went to school. Henriette is older than Suzanne, of course. There was an incident that set them against the Queen. They knew the girl Jeanne de Valois, who later became the Comtesse la Motte.'

Jacob rearranges the papers on the desk and looks up.

'The same la Motte as the woman behind the affair of the diamond necklace?'

She nods. 'The same. Something happened to one of their friends and they blamed the queen. After the business of the necklace, Marie Antoinette refused to acknowledge my sister at court. That's the reason she makes excuses not to attend. She persuaded her husband to take an active part in the Estates General. She cannot bear not to be important.'

She rings the bell and tells the servant to bring wine and biscuits. 'Who is this girl that you wish to find, Jacob?'

He sighs and stands up, crossing the room to where she sits, and looks out of the window. 'In Paris, I often dined in a small tavern, Le Deux Lions, close to my house. The innkeeper, Jules, and his wife had a daughter who helped serve the food. Lucette was a very pretty girl, full of life, but she was of marriageable age and her parents wanted her to find a husband that could provide for her.'

Francine's eyebrows rise in a question he forestalls. 'I should stress that I was not such a man. The girl was approached by a woman I later learned was Suzanne, who provided a letter of introduction to Le Carre—one of the Comptrollers at the court of Versailles. She left the inn, but her parents have had no word of her since. Jules told me that she was in fact his adopted child—that her family gave her to him, along with the lease of his business, which expired the day that she left. He and his wife have returned to domestic service, here in the town. I saw the girl on a cart, with a farmer some days ago, and I hoped Madame Gregory could tell me where she was, so a letter might reach her.'

'If you know that the letter was addressed to Comptroller Le Carre, have you spoken to him?'

He shakes his head. 'I wrote to him and he denied all knowledge of the girl. I requested an audience with him, and he declined. My authority does not reach to the palace of

Versailles, alas.'

The wine and biscuits are brought in by a footman and placed on a small table beside Francine. She asks the servant to pour two glasses and offers one to Jacob, who accepts it, taking a biscuit.

'Tell me,' he says, 'Do you like Madame Gregory?'

She shrugs her thin shoulders. 'She is my sister's friend, not mine. Sandy detests her: he says she is manipulative—she does no favours without expecting something in return. What might she want from this—what is the girl's name, did you say?'

'Lucette. Her name is Lucette.'

'You say she was on a farm cart when you saw her?'

He nods, taking a sip from the wine, which is Grenache and a tad too sweet for his liking.

'If Lucette came to Versailles and took work that meant she was on a farm cart, there is only one place one should look, Jacob.'

'Where do you suggest that place is?' he replies.

'The Queen's Hamlet. The little farm at Le Hameau.'

Chapter Twenty-Five

Lucette is impatient. Her visit to the town was a reminder of her former life, and she fondly takes the new dress out of its bag in the evenings and strokes it as if it were a purring cat. She thinks of how she will wear the dress when next she sees Jacques. He kissed her, long and hard before he returned her to the farmer, and she treasures that memory too.

She knows little about the young man, save that he is one of Le Maitre's printers. The farmer has a brother in Paris who sometimes brings news of the city when he delivers goods or collects eggs to sell. As well as the pamphlets, there are newspapers, which give views of the factions that are rapidly splintering the National Assembly. The farmer disapproves of Desmoulins' *La France Libre*, a republican sheet, which would abolish the monarchy, but approves of Brissot's *Le Patriot Francais,* the mouthpiece of the Girondins, who want France to be governed as Britain is, with the king accountable to the elected assembly. 'Of course,' he says, neither is likely to happen, while the Bourbons are at Versailles.

Lucette is discreet about her young man and Le Maitre,

who she knows works for Marat, who her father says is the most extreme of all.

Prices of grain remain stubbornly high and there is news from Paris of a massacre in the Place de Greves of the Intendent of Paris and his father-in-law, who were suspected of speculating to keep prices too high for most people to pay. The reckoning is coming, the farmer says. There have been peasant revolts around the country, and even only a few miles away, farm labourers have been looting food and attacking the bailiffs.

Lucette asks Avril if they are safe here. The dairymaid gives a hollow laugh. 'This is about the only farm in France that's safe. There are guards nearby, but they're to protect the woman over there,' she says, pointing at the Queen's House.

The days are still long, and one evening, when the farmer and his family are away and Avril has sneaked off to meet a friend, Lucette, alone in the house, and at ease after her duties are finished, washes her hair, cleanses her body and rubs the lanolin she has saved from spinning sheep's wool into her hands to soften them. Then she takes the pink dress out of its bag, and savouring the feel of the fabric, she puts it on, struggling to tie her laces.

It cannot hurt, she tells herself, to put her new dress on to take the air and walk around the Hameau. After all, the Queen is away, and only the animals and servants will see her finery. She picks up a trug. If anyone sees her, she can say she is picking herbs for the garden.

She has no mirror, but she will see her reflection in the pond, which is as still as any looking glass.

With her glossy curls pinned up, and her slender figure accented by the tight bodice, she has no idea of how lovely she looks. Only her shabby little shoes let her down. She steps daintily out of the dairy, holding her skirts free of the cobbles and imagines herself a fine lady as she walks to the pond, trug over her arm.

She is dismayed to find she is not alone. A woman sits by the pond, a book in her hands. Lucette decides to take a chance, only for a moment, to view her reflection. As she looks at the pretty girl on the surface of the dark water, the woman looks up and gives a strangled cry. 'Otillie?'

Dressed in white, with unpowdered hair, Lucette doesn't at first recognise Marie Antoinette. The seconds tick by before she sinks into the deepest curtsy she has ever made in her life.

She is utterly flustered. She knows she is not allowed to look at the queen, and certainly not allowed to speak, unless addressed directly.

'No, your Majesty, my name is Lucette. I am so sorry—I must go back...'

'You wear her dress and you have her dear face. Who are you?'

'I am a servant at your farm, your Majesty. The dress was a gift from a friend. It is not new.'

She realises to her horror that the queen is in tears. Lucette turns and gathering up her skirts, she runs back to the farm.

Watching from the other side of the Hameau, Suzanne Gregory smiles. She could not have arranged things better if she had tried.

Chapter Twenty-Six

Jeannie wakes up each morning tired out by uneasy dreams. Disturbing dreams in which her secret is discovered. When she and Johnny began their deception, in Aberdeen, the Reverend had been teaching them to appreciate the works of Shakespeare. Of course, it was King Lear and Hamlet that he used to teach the beauty of the language and the philosophy contained in each play. Johnny preferred the more bloodthirsty Macbeth, while it was the dark comedy of Twelfth Night that appealed to Jeannie. Like Viola and Sebastian, Jonathon and Jeannie were almost identical twins. What better than to emulate the plot to allow Johnny the chance to follow his interest in politics and to educate a sister who otherwise would be confined to housekeeping and knitting.

Recently, she has been taken for her brother when she has been abroad on the streets on business. Some of the men who have called out 'Citizen Jacques!' are unsavoury sorts, clad in *sans culottes* and she worries about the company he is keeping. These are the ruffians she witnessed at the Café Foy and they are easily stirred up. They prowl the streets: hyenas baying for blood. Worse still, she has witnessed women joining in the violence, helping to build barricades of furniture, stones and anything that they can lay hands on, and physically attacking anyone who speaks against the actions of the mob.

She has avoided going to hear the King's speech—she fears the volatility of the mob. When roused, they are drunk on violence and their power to do harm. She tells herself she is cautious rather than cowardly, but she rarely leaves the house unless it is unavoidable.

Johnny has changed his appearance: he has cropped his light brown hair and wears the loose trousers or *sans culotte* of a working man, with a short jacket and red neckerchief. A blood red knitted cap is stuffed into a pocket. The look is raffish but ruffianly, and it suits him.

'Why the change of clothes?' she asks, fingering the coarse sleeve of the jacket.

'Le Maitre wants me in the crowd, now. I can be useful there,' he says. His eyes shine with zeal.

She has seen what happens in the crowd, and it makes her feel sick at the thought that her twin is orchestrating the violence. Had she not agreed to change places with him, she might have prevented some of the trouble.

However, the deaths in the Places de Greves have not gone unnoticed, and Jeannie wonders if the change is a disguise, should he be identified as an agent provocateur.

Men being torn to pieces by the mob. Women beaten and left for dead. If this is the world her brother has created, she wants none of it.

Throughout August, she writes to Jacob at Versailles of the violence in Paris. She tries not to betray how scared she is, and to make her letters about the work she does on his behalf. He replies:

Dear Jean

Julie MP Adams

My duties at the Assembly require my full attention, and it is my wish that you continue to run the practice. I should prefer that you deal with existing clients and business, rather than taking on new work for the time being.

I give you authority to issue invoices and take payment, and in recognition of the additional work you must do, you will receive payment of two livres a month.

Furthermore, this letter gives you authority to carry out investigations on my behalf.

I have a task for you, which is a matter of urgency. I want you to visit Passy. There is a girls' boarding school where Francine Geddes and her sister, Henriette were educated. Find out the names of all those pupils, around similar age, born between 1755 and 1760, and if any of those girls subsequently entered the convent of Longchamps as novices. Visit me here to collect a letter of introduction.

Should a woman who calls herself Suzanne Gregory or Gregoire approach you, exercise caution in your dealings with her.

Your obedient servant,

Jacob A Rose.

She reads the letter twice. He trusts her enough to give her independence and to carry out an investigation on his behalf. Passy, she learns is close to Paris, and the convent of Longchamps is close to Versailles. A day or so out of the heat and tension of Paris, she decides is what she needs.

Chapter Twenty-Seven

August, 28th, 1789

Jacob tires of his hosts. A visitor to their home, calling on Henriette, is accompanied by little Etienne, the page from the colonies. A ridiculous vain woman who has never known a day's hardship in her life, reaches for a marron glace and declares herself delighted with the boy. As her friends in Paris say her page is the height of fashion, she asks Henriette and her husband to find one for them too. The very thought that a member of the Assembly is trafficking in slaves sickens Jacob in a way it did not before.

Perhaps he has imbibed the spirit of the Assembly?

He attends meetings in a clerical capacity to set down the *'Rights of Man and the Citizen'* document that is drawn up by Lafayette, based on the American model. Jacob recalls that the American Declaration of Independence was inspired by the 1320 document drawn up by the Abbot of Arbroath Abbey, in Captain Cargill's home port. He must remind the man of that, when he returns from his next voyage.

The senior members of the Assembly have Jacob at their

beck and call this month, with barely a minute to himself as one edict after another is published.

On the fourth of August, as predicted, to everyone's relief, the King recalls Necker and appoints reforming ministers to serve under him. At the same time the Assembly abolishes the privileges and feudal rights of the nobility. These are huge changes but Jacob fears they are too little and too late. There's talk in Paris of Marat causing yet more trouble. Jacob has Marat's '*A plot uncovered to lull the people to sleep,*' on his desk. Jean brought it on his recent visit—to collect the letter of authority for his visit to Passy.

'Marat is stirring up the *sans culottes*. I've seen the violence for myself,' the clerk says. 'He wants much more than this Assembly will deliver.'

Jacob shows the drafts of two declarations: freedom of religious opinions and freedom of speech. 'Will these appease the *sans culottes?*' he asks.

Jean replies, 'Freedom of religion is fine if you're a Huguenot; not so fine if you're a Jew. The mob have already claimed freedom of speech. The *sans culottes* are moving faster than the Assembly can issue edicts. They're dangerous. You haven't seen them at their worst: I have.

'What of the King?' Jean asks. 'What powers does he have over the Assembly now, if the nobles have lost their privileges?'

He has a point. With Marat and his friends demanding more and more change, how long before they demand the abolition of the monarchy altogether? He should pay attention to his clerk's reports—the lad is clearly alarmed by what is happening in Paris.

Jacob's head hurts. His fingers are cramped from writing, and he needs some air. He stands up and stretches his hands above his head. He will take an evening walk. He washes the ink from his hands and gathers his hat, coat and cane.

The Scottish Agent

The August evening is warm and the streets are full of people who have had the same idea. The Assembly meetings are long and drawn out, leaving only evenings for exercise. He walks swiftly, doffing his hat to those he meets, and spotting those he recognises. There are fewer silk clad nobles in the streets, this month. Artois was the first of many aristocrats to take flight, and many of the remaining courtiers are holed up in the palace, desperately trying to find a way to limit the powers of the Assembly. Most of those he meets are the same people he sees in the meetings, but he notices men from the Embassies, who are taking a keen interest in what is going on.

He reaches Mercier's house and makes his way to the stables, where he knows he will find Jules.

Chapter Twenty-Eight

The Abbe Caron is not what Jean expects. The boarding school at Passy is run by nuns, with the superintendent and Latin master a junior member of the clergy. Caron is young and handsome and admits he has been in post for only five years. He agrees to see Jean, in the parlour of the rectory.

Raised in the Church of Scotland, Jean is still suspicious of the Catholic clergy, but the rectory is very similar to the Reverend Milne's house, except for the *prie dieu* in the corner, with a suffering Christ on the cross. The abbe scrutinises her letter of authority and says, 'Let me summon Sister Marthe. She oversees the boarders and keeps our archives. She will be of greater help to you than I can be.' He rings a bell and when a nun comes, he whispers something. The woman nods and goes through a door into the school.

The abbe offers a glass of home-made lemonade, which Jean accepts gratefully after the dusty ride from the city. It is refreshing and tangy and she wants to ask for the recipe, but just in time remembers that the young man she appears to be would do no such thing.

Sister Marthe appears twenty minutes later, apologising.

The Scottish Agent

'I was taking a class and unable to leave them before Sister Bernadette came to take the next lesson. Girls can be boisterous if left to their own devices.'

Jean—reminding herself that she is indeed Jean the clerk and not Jeannie the girl, enquires as to the subject the nun was teaching,

'It was a lesson on the Catechism. The girls will be confirmed before Christmas. Those intending to enter the convent have lessons in Latin. The others, whose parents hope they will make good marriages, study needlework, and deportment.'

The nun leads Jean through the door and into a large square hallway, with galleries above. She walks close to the wall, hands folded within her sleeves until they reach a door, which she unlocks. She ushers Jean into an office with a small desk and shelves filled with ledgers. She deliberately leaves the door wide open.

'I understand you wish to know about the girls who were boarders here twenty years ago? What, might I ask is your interest in these ladies?' Sister Marthe's face is inscrutable, showing nothing more than a pleasant and serene half smile.

Jean has prepared for this. 'A client is drawing up a Will and is looking for a lady whom he wishes to make his heir. He knows that she attended the school here, and that she then was bound for the convent at Longchamps. He has only this information, and I am to furnish him with the list of names, and to tell him something of her school days. I would like to see your roll for each year from 1767–1771. The person I am looking for would have been around sixteen or seventeen years of age at that time.'

The nun crosses to the shelves and runs her fingers across several volumes. The ledgers are bound in leather and Jean can see that each covers a period of three years, with the dates stamped in gold leaf on the spine. She uses both hands to draw the heavy book from the shelf, before setting it on the table, and opening it at one entry—for 1770. She indicates Jean may sit at the desk and opens the inkwell. There is a quill set ready, and Jean smiles thanks.

The nun goes to the window, looking out over the school gardens. It is recess and a dozen girls are playing with a ball, throwing it and reciting a rhyme. It is a carefree scene.

'If I read out the list of names, would you be able to tell me what you know of their lives after they left here?' Jean asks.

She reads: 'Henriette Lacarriere and Francine Lacarriere'. These are the names that Jacob gave her as a place to start.

Marthe replies, 'Their parents were bourgeois, with land and money. Francine is the wife of a Scottish merchant, and her older sister married an ennobled landowner. Francine was a good girl; her sister kept company with troublemakers.'

'Marie Fabre?'

'Marie had poor health and died a year after she left school. She was a good child. She is with Our Lord.'

'Isolde Coutard?'

'Isolde entered the convent at Longchamps and is their mistress of novices. She is a good scholar.'

'Jeanne de Valois?'

Sister Marthe's composure has vanished. 'We rue the day that girl arrived at the school. She was brought here when her parents failed her. Her father was a descendent of kings, but her mother was a servant girl, and she was nothing but trouble. Always sly, plotting some mischief or other, breaking all our rules. She was bound for the convent—after all there was no dowry for her, but she managed to dupe the Comte de la Motte—another scoundrel—into marriage. She brought shame on the school.'

Jean looks up, deliberately assuming a blank expression. 'What did she do to provoke such disgrace?'

The Scottish Agent

'You have heard of the affair of the diamond necklace? That woman and her husband broke the law for personal gain. For an alumnus of this school to have been branded as a thief and a liar and to be sentenced to life imprisonment in the Salpetiere prison? Parents would not send their daughters to any school that nurtured such a viper in their bosom.' The nun is tugging at the fabric of her sleeve, and Jean notices her knuckles are white with rage.

'Suzanne Malraux?'

'Suzanne was, like her friend Jeanne, a troubled girl. She broke rules, but where Jeanne was openly mutinous, she was sly, and always able to blame someone else for the trouble she caused. She married a wealthy man, but I do not recall his name?'

Jean thinks this might be the Suzanne Gregory that Jacob warned her about.

'Otillie de Saint Combs?'

The nun remains silent. She has turned her back on Jean, who waits for her to speak. Jean writes her notes, scratching the quill across the paper. When she looks up, she realises that Sister Marthe's shoulders are trembling, and she is crying softly, swallowing sobs, and struggling to maintain her composure.

Jean fights an impulse to go to her, to offer comfort, but remembers that Jean the clerk may do no such thing. Instead, she waits silently until the sobs subside and the nun speaks.

'When one takes the veil, one is supposed to set aside the life one lived before. Otillie's mother was my good friend. She died when her child was very young, and the father, a soldier, away at the American wars, placed her in our school and asked us to raise her. A nobleman, the Vicomte Pellegrin became his patron, and when Otillie was fifteen years of age, Pellegrin requested her hand in marriage. She would leave us and accept a place at Court, to be a lady in waiting to the

Dauphine. The Vicomte was extremely powerful and it was a match beyond the girl's expectations. After all, with little dowry, she would have been destined for a convent, or a modest marriage.'

Jean listens, nodding, then asks, 'Why did her name upset you, Sister?'

'At Court, the girl was beloved of the Dauphine, who offered to continue her education with music lessons. Otillie proved talented, and the Vicomte was delighted at first that she was favoured by the Dauphine—the future queen.'

'Something happened?' Jean asks.

'The Vicomte was over forty years old. He was a widower, having had two wives who died. The music master, a young Italian, was nineteen years old, and charming. Otillie married him in secret, in the church she attended when she was here. They hid the match, and returned to court, to resume their duties, until such time as they had the courage to tell the Vicomte and her father.'

'I begged them to run away, to leave France, Monsieur. Otillie was carrying a child, and her husband loved her so. She was a brave girl, and a good woman, who did not run from trouble—and that was her undoing.'

'The Vicomte and her father forced the annulment of the marriage. They threw the young father in prison, and they took Otillie to the convent. She was forced into a religious life against her will.'

Jean asks, 'And the child?'

The nun raises her hand to her face and wipes tears on her sleeve. 'The child was given to servants, to be brought up as their own. Otillie was not allowed to know where she was.'

Jean writes on the paper.

There is another dozen names on the list, but Jean knows she has the information that Jacob needs. This matches the

The Scottish Agent

story that Jules told. The child of Otillie must be Lucette.

Chapter Twenty-Nine

August 29th, 1789

Tonight's meeting, held in the back room of an inn, was angry. Marat, his skin condition flaring up, has been in a bad mood, anxious to leave and return to his medicinal bath. He is planning a new newspaper, which Le Maitre already has started to prepare.

The Revolution is divided, between those Girondins who would be content to follow the British way of government, with an upper and lower house, and a Royal veto, and the radicals who would dispense with the court and nobility altogether and rule as the Americans do. A country where there is equality and one gains position through merit, rather than through any accident of birth. Jacques, of course knows which he would prefer and says so, loudly. Le Maitre applauds him.

Camille Desmoulins plans a demonstration tomorrow, at the Palais Royal. He wants them to rouse the mob tonight, and to prepare to throw up barricades, should the troops decided to charge against them. Jacques is eager to start, but

Le Maitre gestures to him to remain, when the gathering breaks up.

At first, Jacques is impatient, but the arrival of Suzanne Gregory and her husband, who is rarely seen at their councils, makes him sit down again.

Desmoulins outlines their objectives for tomorrow. They are to block any royal veto, and they are to force the King and Court to move to Paris.

Jacques says, 'Why would you want them in Paris? Isn't it better to keep them at a distance and to use that as an excuse to be angry at them?'

Desmoulins shakes his head. 'Paris is where we want them to be. Louis XIV moved the court outside of Paris, because it was too easy for a rebellion against the king to flare up in the city. At Versailles, he controlled the nobles through ridiculous etiquette—to this day, one cannot be armed at court. He made himself and his heirs into gods, far removed from the people. They've lived in pampered luxury long enough. The people need to see them for what they really are—a fat fool and a silly spouse.'

Le Maitre addresses Suzanne. 'What news of the girl?'

'Marie Antoinette set eyes on her a month ago. She wore her mother's wedding dress and the Queen thought she was looking at a ghost. If we expose her part in the suffering of the Prisoner Valenti, the mob will take against her even more.'

'I will not be content until we see the back of the Bourbons,' Suzanne's husband declares. 'They live in comfort while Paris tightens its belt.'

'Just a pity you don't speak like this in the Assembly,' Desmoulins says, picking up his coat and brushing an imaginary speck of dust from the sleeve. 'Actions speak louder than words. I shall bid you goodnight. I go to prepare for tomorrow.'

Le Maitre calls for a bottle of brandy and takes a seat at a table, pulling out chairs for Suzanne and her husband, and for Jacques.

'How is the Prisoner Valenti?' Suzanne asks.

'He's impatient to see his wife and his daughter,' Le Maitre says. 'After twenty years, wouldn't you be? What have you done with the girl?'

'I've told the farmer that she has a lover in the town and that he is to keep a close watch on her, and not let her out of his sight. It appears that we are not the only ones interested in her.'

Le Maitre raises an eyebrow and lifts the bottle to pour a measure into each glass.

'That tiresome usher, Jacob Rose, asked me to find her. I have instructed Le Carre to refuse to help him. I have suggested that he has questionable motives, and that the girl might be in danger.'

'What exactly is your plan?' Le Maitre asks, raising his glass to his lips and drinking, with obvious satisfaction.

'We choose our moment carefully to arrange a public reunion for Prisoner of the Bastille Valenti and the girl.'

'And her mother?' Jacques asks.

'That is more complicated,' she replies. 'We choose a moment when the Queen's part in their misery can be most powerful.' There is steel in her voice, and her gloved hand grips the glass tightly as she raises it in a toast, 'To the downfall and damnation of Madam Deficit!'

Chapter Thirty

September 1st, 1789

'Ah, Jacob, my friend, excellent news from Paris,' Mirabeau declares, as he walks to the Assembly with the usher. The uprising planned for the thirtieth failed, sending Desmoulins, Marat and their followers back to the shadows. 'Where the lot of them belong, but I doubt they shall remain. Desmoulins seems to have found his voice?'

Jacob recalls earlier meetings with the young man when he had been studying law. 'Didn't he have a stammer?'

'He loses it when he rouses the rabble, it would appear.'

Jacob agrees, but inwardly the prospect that the King and the Assembly might have moved to Paris, allowing him to quit his lodgings with Henriette and her husband, had cheered him up. He misses his little house and the company of young Jean, and a quiet supper in an inn, at the end of a day's work. It remains his intention to quit as an usher at the earliest opportunity. He says as much to Mirabeau, who says, 'Yes, yes, but...' and then holds forth about the Constitution Committee of the Assembly's proposal to create a two

House Parliament with a royal veto. Like the British house of Commons and House of Lords, a Constitutional Monarchy. It will please the Girondins, he argues, and stop the radicals from pursuing a republic.

The day ahead holds much work for Jacob. He must work on administration matters, but Geddes is due to visit, and he must give the merchant the report on events that he will convey to Lord Dorset at the British Embassy.

Jacob reflects his role as a spy within the Assembly can only last so long before he is discovered. He had letters today from Henry Dundas and his cousin, George Rose, which, as instructed, he burned after reading. Not only must he report back on the activities of the Assembly, but he must seek to influence it.

'The British government takes no pleasure in the predicament of King Louis, despite his past support for the American rebels. However, should a wave of revolutionary fervour remove a King, this would present a threat to His Majesty's government, if that fervour crossed borders. On no account must the Paris mob be allowed to unseat the monarchy.'

They ask much of a plain Paris notary who does not seek to be the centre of attention.

Mirabeau is speaking, and he realises he has not been listening. 'Have you found the child you were seeking, Jacob? Was Le Carre of any help?'

Jacob shakes his head. In fact, in the meeting he finally secured, Le Carre was anything but helpful, suggesting that Monsieur Rose' motives for seeking out the girl were sinister and against the girl's best interest, 'Even if I knew such a girl existed, which I do not.' Le Carre, powdered and bewigged and dressed in satin livery feigned a moral superiority which Jacob suspected was a front.

Jacob spent the previous Sunday walking to the Hameau, and calling on the farmer. He recognised the fellow from the cart, but when he asked for Lucette, the man replied he had offered her transport only a short way along the road, and that no, she did not work on the farm.

Jacob said, 'I have had a long walk today, and a glass of water would be most welcome. Might I come in?'

The farmer called for his wife, and a plain woman in a drab dress and voluminous apron scuttled to the door with a cup of water, which she offered with a bobbed curtsy.

He declined the money that Jacob offered for the location where the girl had left the cart. 'I do not recall, Monsieur.'

It was obvious the man was lying.

Jacob drank the water slowly, looking around him at the outside of the little farm.

As he handed the cup back and turned to go, he said, loudly and clearly, 'Should you meet the young woman again, please give her this message. Her father, Jules, and her mother live in the town of Versailles, and are servants to Monsieur Mercier. They would dearly like to see their daughter. That, alone, is my reason for visiting today. Thank you for your kind hospitality, Monsieur. I bid you good day.'

He loitered at the Hameau, taking in the exquisite little buildings which belonged to a Fragonard idyll and bore little resemblance to the real farms where the labourers often went to bed hungry. He thought that the very existence of this place, created for one woman's pet project was the epitome of royal insensitivity to the people they ruled. Somewhere, inside the confection that was the Queen's House, Marie Antoinette would be sitting with her ladies, oblivious to the intentions of Marat and Desmoulins.

Chapter Thirty-One

Two small children hurtle through the gate of the convent, almost knocking Jean over, as they run towards the gardens. They are followed by a blowsy woman, curls askew and shouting for them to stop.

Jean has expected the rigour of a closed order convent, but the outer part of Longchamps Abbey, it appears is little more than a pensione, where distressed gentlefolk, mostly widows and younger women reside for a modest payment, often provided by the court.

If Ottilie de Saint Combs is here, she will surely not be so miserable?

Jean has written to the Abbey, requesting an audience. The reply, from Reverend Mother Marie V Jeanne Jouy, instructs her to report to the front lodge.

Longchamps, or the Convent of the Humility of the Blessed Virgin, belongs to the order of the Poor Clares. Jean sees little poverty here, and no humility.

There is, however, a building within the convent where those sisters who have taken the veil and retreated from the world reside. None of these sisters venture beyond the cloister, and they have little contact with the paying residents or indeed anyone beyond their walls.

The Abbess suggests they take a turn around the physic garden, which has high stone walls, and where they will be free from eavesdroppers. 'There was a police report into the Abbey some years ago, and I regret to say that the criticism of our lodgers was largely true. Even the young men who dressed as a dancing bear to visit the Bedelles sisters. We have addressed these matters, but there are always those who wish to close the abbey down. We must not give them cause to do so.'

Jean thinks of the ruined abbey of Arbroath—once the centre of power for Scotland's clergy and now housing a thread factory in the abbot's house. Those who wish to close churches and abbeys are often those who profit from their lands.

'In your letter, Monsieur Rose, you mentioned several names—young ladies who came to us from the convent school at Passy. You will have met Sister Marthe?'

Jean nods. They reach a bench surrounded by bushy lavender plants. Bees are buzzing around the late blooming flowers and the scent that rises is calming. The abbess tucks her hands into her sleeves and sits down, indicating the seat next to her, and Jean, perches on the bench. 'The bees are busy and will not sting you unless you disturb them.'

The Abbess explains that her work with plants, as a healer, means that she lives in the outer part of the abbey, with the sisters who run the pensione, while the closed order is led by Sister Anne. 'Two of the names in your letter resided in the pensione, as they were young women waiting for husbands, and unsuited to the monastic life. They were both here three years after the police report during the time of my predecessor. She was relieved when Jeanne de Valois and Suzanne Malraux left us.'

She takes a deep breath. 'The lavender has the power to remove anxiety, and those names can only cause malign feelings. The other names, Isolde Coutard and Ottilie de Saint Combs are a different matter. Isolde chose the secluded life and is our dear Sister Anne. Ottilie did not choose to take the veil, but had it forced upon her by her father. My predecessor fought to keep her with the healers, as she was with child. We could not have a woman give birth in the closed house without the aid of a midwife. She begged for mercy for the girl, to have her live in the pensione with her child until the father forgave her, or her young husband was released from prison. We are not a cruel order.'

Jean asks, 'What became of the woman and her child?'

'Ottilie gave birth to a daughter shortly before the Christmas of 1771. She was barely sixteen years of age, and her labour was long and dangerous—so dangerous that we gave her extreme unction after the baby was born. We feared for her life.'

Jean gets up from the bench, but the nun says, 'Sit please, monsieur. Ottilie did not die in childbirth and lived to nurse her daughter for the first three months of her life. Her father and his patron refused to let the child remain with her and sent a servant and his wife to take the baby. They refused to say where the child was going, but I bribed the woman to write to me. I hoped this would be sufficient to give Ottilie hope.'

'She entered the closed order and took the veil, and as they cut her hair, when she took her final vows, she screamed—such a scream. Then she made no sound at all.'

Jean says. 'It is important. I need to see her. Her daughter's life may be in danger, and there are matters I need to discuss.'

The abbess says, 'She is not here. If you wish to see her, then you must go to the asylum of Charenton. Ottilie stopped eating two years ago, and it was not God's will that we allowed her to take her own life. They care for her there, and they keep her safe from those in the world who would wish to hurt her.'

'Monsieur, others have come looking for Ottilie, and I did not give them this information. I recognised Suzanne, and I know she has bad intentions towards Ottilie.'

'Might I ask why you trust me?' Jean asks.

'You work for a good man, whom people trust, but please be careful with what I have told you, I beseech you.'

Chapter Thirty-Two

Jacques reaches to the lintel for the key to Jacob's house, but it is missing. He saw his twin leave earlier and he intends to read her correspondence. He pulls the skeleton key from his pocket and looking over his shoulder as he fiddles at the lock, after only a few minutes, he opens the door.

His sister keeps the shutters closed when she is abroad and he opens them, allowing the sunshine of a September morning to creep into the room. He prowls the parlour, shuffling through the papers on his sister's small desk by the window, disappointed to find only a lease agreement, a widow's Last Will and Testament and invoices ready to be delivered.

The folder on Jacob's desk offers up very little—more documents pertaining to the business and nothing from the Assembly, but as the older man is resident in Versailles, he expected little else. Using the skeleton key, he opens the desk drawer, and draws out a bundle of documents bound together with red tape and seals. He slides the papers free, laying them on the table in front of him, then, crosses to the cupboard and helps himself to a drink.

The Scottish Agent

He is still reading several hours later when Jean the clerk returns. She removes the hat and coat, shaking the dust of the streets off the outer garment. She shows no surprise at his presence.

'I presume this is not a social call,' she says, taking a seat in the comfortable armchair Jacob uses for clients, and crossing her legs. 'I hope you have not damaged the desk drawer.'

'Might I ask what you are looking for? I might be able to help you.' Her tone is polite but guarded. 'Are you in need of a lawyer? Jacob has told me not to take on new business,'

He looks towards the door. There's a woman leaning against the frame, tapping the riding crop in her hand against her leg. Jeannie glances at her, trying to place where she has seen her before.

'So, Jeannie Alexandra Rose, we finally meet. Your brother has told me a great deal about you. I suspect you and I have a great deal in common. It appears we have both been looking for a friend of mine.'

'It would be such a shame if Jacob were to find out his clerk is a woman. What will happen to you if it becomes common knowledge? A girl who chooses to dress and live as a man? I suspect there are laws. Or perhaps your brother could say you were mad and send you to an asylum?'

Johhny moves behind his sister and his fingers dig into her arms, pinning her to the chair. Suzanne Gregory has a half smile on her face as she brushes Jeannie's face with the end of the whip.

'A few strokes of this could ruin your looks forever. Do you really wish to take that risk?'

This, Jeannie realises is the person the nuns warned her against, and she knows what she wants. She struggles under her brother's grip. She tries to turn to glare at him, but his fingers dig into her shoulders,

Julie MP Adams

'So, Jeannie. What's it to be? Do we expose you as a woman, and have Jacob throw you out on the streets? Or does your brother lock you up as a lunatic? Perhaps you prefer to be silent and have us torture you until you tell us what we wish to know? I should tell you how useful Jacques here is with his hands. He's a skilled printer, but he's even better at inflicting pain. Do you really want to take that risk?'

Chapter Thirty-Three

Jacob's voice—drifts up to the attic where Lucette is locked in. Since that night when the Queen mistook her for whoever Ottilie is, she's been kept under lock and key. The farmer accused her of stealing the pink frock: 'how could a poor farm girl afford a Court dress?'

Servants don't dally around the Queen. They do not call attention to themselves. If Lucette is let go without a reference, she will be finished. No employer would hire her—she would be damaged goods. Worse still, she was seen with a young man, and the farmer now doubts her good character. She is to stay in this dusty attic with the spiders and the mice, until he lets her out, and from the tone of his voice that will not be soon.

That night, when she fled from the Queen, she dashed into the dairy and up to her attic. She tore the dress off, alarmed both by her boldness and by the longing in Marie Antoinette's voice.

She heard the farmer and his family return home, their happy voices, and their footsteps in the yard. She heard, too, the woman on horseback ride into the yard, dismount and talk with the farmer. The woman's voice was muffled, but there was something familiar about it, that Lucette wished she could remember.

That was when he climbed to the attic and ordered her to come down and bring her things with her. Still in shock, she did as she was told, meekly.

She's been in the farmhouse loft since, her food delivered by the farmer's sullen wife. The woman looks at Lucette with suspicion and does not speak a single word to her. She has no candle, and when the sun sets, she throws herself on the single blanket that serves for her bed, weeping. She's lost track of the days. She only knows that she is scared, alone, often hungry and doesn't understand what she has done so wrong to deserve this imprisonment.

Now, hearing Monsieur Rose's familiar voice telling the farmer where her parents are is too much for her and she hammers at the window, as he walks away. Each step is a reminder of how miserable she feels.

Chapter Thirty-Four

Jacob is distraught. Sandy Geddes tells him that Cargill, calling at his house found the building not only unlocked, but ransacked and no sign of his clerk. Jean's little trunk is missing. It is assumed the clerk has taken the money from the premises and left in a hurry. Geddes and Cargill ask if any neighbour saw the lad leaving but meet only silence. The great fear that has gripped Paris since the storming of the Bastille makes everyone suspicious and scared for their own safety.

Sandy, riding with Cargill to give the news to Jacob, laments that the lad he hired has deserted him. 'It's my fault. I should have realised that a troublemaker cannot change his ways.'

Jacob, in contrast denies that his clerk could do any such thing. He's trusted Jean with the business and has had no complaints about the boy's work. This, he suspects, relates to the mission he sent the lad on, to investigate Suzanne Gregory. He declares his faith in Jean, but there is something niggling at the back of his mind.

'Do you know the whereabouts of the sister, Geddes?

She might hold the key to what has become of Jean. All he would tell me was that she was with good people who took care of her, and I was not to worry.'

He voices his suspicion also of the farmer at the Hameau, and Geddes listens thoughtfully. 'If Jules went to the place and demanded his daughter back, he would have every right to search the farm. Have you considered taking him with you?'

'I plan to do so at the first opportunity, but my work requires me to be at the disposal of the Assembly and I do not know when that will be.' He looks up as a footman enters the room. 'A message from Paris, sir. It is to be given into your hands only.'

Jacob recognises the seal as identical to his own and frowns. His signet is on his finger—he did not leave it in Paris. He breaks the seal and reads the letter.

To Monsieur Rose

I will instruct this letter is delivered directly into your hands. You were correct in your belief that Suzanne Gregory is a person with evil intent. The Abbess of Longchamps confirms that Suzanne Gregory came to the convent with Jeanne de Valois, later La Motte, and Ottilie de Saint Combs after leaving the school at Passy. Both girls were among the witnesses at a clandestine marriage between Ottilie and the music master, Gianfranco Valenti. The marriage was annulled and Ottilie placed in the closed order within Longchamps. The child of the marriage, a girl, was taken by servants of the Vicomte who would care for her as their own. This I suspect is connected to our young friend, Lucette. I learned Ottilie was moved from Longchamps and will investigate further. I cannot say more, for fear I have been followed, and I do not wish to place the person we seek in further danger. I will visit when I have learned more.

Your humble and obedient servant,
Jean Rose'

The Scottish Agent

Jacob shows the letter to Sandy Geddes, who takes a pair of spectacles from his pocket, and puts them on to read it.

'Does that sound like my clerk intended to abscond?' he asks Geddes, who shakes his head.

Cargill takes the letter from Sandy and reads it quickly. There's a curious expression on his face.

'This isn't the lad's writing. Both he and his sister wrote in the ship's log. The lad had a very bold hand, and I'd know it anywhere. 'This writing isn't his. It's his sister's.'

A chance encounter in the town. The boy who accompanied Bailly and Guillotin in the Tennis Court. He has seen him only occasionally since.

Jacob says, 'Several months ago, I saw a boy in the town here, whom I mistook for my clerk. How close was the resemblance between the two?'

Cargill goes to the sideboard and pours himself a glass of brandy, sniffing at the glass before raising it to his lips.

'They're similar in build, both small of frame and not very well fed, but the lad was a bit taller, and his features were sharper. I suppose, if the girl wore a lad's clothing, she might pass for him, but her face would be smooth.'

Francine has been listening at the door, and the hem of her dress whispers her presence as she moves to stand beside her husband. 'I think it might be prudent to speak with your laundress, Jacob. There are things that no woman would be able to conceal.'

Geddes and Cargill set off on horseback, leaving Jacob and Francine to follow in a hired carriage. Jacob wishes he was riding, as the coach bumps over potholes and Francine clings to the silken cords, to avoid falling into his lap.

They arrive in Paris in the early evening and seek out the washerwoman in her cottage. She looks alarmed at the three well-dressed men and the elegant woman with them.

Francine says, 'Leave this to me,' and disappears into the little house.

She emerges half an hour later, and accompanies them to Jacob's house, where a locksmith has changed the locks on the door. Sandy tells them where he instructed the replacement key to be left. 'You'll need to see what's missing, Jacob.'

'Only you, Jacob, would not see what is right in front of your eyes,' Francine says.

'Marie Claude told me that she noticed spots of blood on the clerk's sheets several times—mainly a month apart. She knew that Jean did some personal washing in the scullery and was secretive about drying it, taking it up to the attic.'

Geddes says, 'Why wouldn't the woman tell you, Jacob?'

Francine says, 'She felt sorry for Jean. It seems that the brother has been the source of much of the trouble in this city. He is an apprentice of the man they call Le Maitre and was seen leading the riot at the Palais Royal with Desmoulins. He calls himself Jacques.'

Jacob puts his head in his hands. 'If he's kidnapped my clerk—his sister, she is in danger. What am I to do about this?'

Chapter Thirty-Five

Jacques expects a great deal more credit than the Gregorys and Le Maitre are giving him. After all, he's led them closer to their prize. He followed Jeanne to the school at Passy and to the convent at Longchamps, and he knows that the nuns were much more welcoming to the young clerk than they were to Suzanne, whom they both recognised and feared.

Of late, Suzanne has avoided him. He misses their assignations. In a moment of weakness, in her arms, he let slip the arrangement he'd made with his sister, and now he has a twinge of guilt. When he kept his secrets, she couldn't get enough of him.

Walking in the Luxembourg gardens, he sees the woman he loves and attempts to take Suzanne's hand to caress the palm with his thumb, but she shakes him off and places two yards between them. When he asks the reason for her coldness, she pushes up the sleeve of her gown. There are bruises.

'Who did that? Your husband?'

Her face is a series of masks—loathing, suspicion and something he cannot define, yet sends shivers through his spine.

'My lover.'

There is confusion in his eyes. 'You know I would not harm you,' he begins.

She laughs, but there is little mirth in it. 'You? You were a mere distraction: a means to an end. It is over.'

The words sting more than any slap. He grabs her by the shoulders and kisses her roughly, but his actions are seen by others and an old man approaches and strikes him with his cane.

'Ruffian! *Sans culottes*! How dare you touch a lady of quality. Desist! Constable!'

The blows are without any real force, but Jacques steps back, suddenly aware of how it must look. In his short jacket and loose trousers he looks the part of a lout, while Suzanne in her smart serge gown is the very picture of outraged bourgeoisie.

When Le Maitre, meets them at the end of the path, Suzanne takes his arm and says, 'Send your dog back to the kennels, Cheri. He forgets his place.'

The older man says, 'Who told you to leave the print shop? Marat needs you there now. Run along.'

Of course, he is needed. Marat's new publication, *'L'ami du peuple'* is almost ready to go to print and he must rally those who will deliver it to the readers tomorrow. It goes further than any of them have dared to go so far, attacking the King, accusing Necker and his ministers of betraying the people. Above all else, he demands the Assembly—which has declared an interest to relocating to Tours, instead to be established in Paris, where fervour for change is loudest.

Mirabeau and Necker, along with his sister's employer, Jacob the Usher need to know that they are now the servants of the people—and that change is going to be at a faster pace than they could ever dream.

Chapter Thirty-Six

Jeannie looks from the attic window, over the rooftops of Paris, in despair.

She wasn't fully conscious when they took her from Jacob's house to this place—which, from what she can tell is five storeys high. A fall from the roof would be certain death. They've taken her clothes away, and she's left only in the threadbare woman's shift that was folded at the bottom of her trunk. It's an old one and it is tight under her armpits. The trunk and its contents are in the possession of her captors, who are no doubt going through it, in search of the intelligence she has steadfastly refused to pass to them.

She gives a silent thanks to the courier who agreed to take her written report to Jacob—for it to be placed in his hands, sealed. She's never used her father's signet in previous correspondence, and she hopes he grasps the significance of this. She's been aware that someone was on her trail, and she half expected a visit from her brother. Now that she's seen who he's kept company with, she is even more determined to keep her mouth shut.

If she hadn't been told of the malice that Suzanne

Gregory is capable of, she would have known it anyway from the woman's voice and her threats. Jeannie rubs her thin shoulders, where her brother's grasp left bruises. There's a mark too, across the left side of her face, where the woman struck her with the riding crop, splitting her lip and drawing blood.

She hasn't seen Suzanne since she was thrown in this attic, but she knows that it is only a matter of time, before there's another encounter. She knows this is only the start.

She contemplates her future—if indeed she has one. She's seen what happens to anyone who gets in the way of Jacques and his fanatical friends.

If she did escape, dressed only in her thin linen shift, she wouldn't last long before she would be cast into a prison or a madhouse. Where would she go? Jacob is a good master, but even if she finds her way back to him, she knows he's too proper to harbour an unmarried young woman under his roof. Her days as an apprentice notary are over, and she finds that the greatest loss of all. If she survives, she can only hope for a different existence as a servant, or governess, or wife.

The door is unbolted, and a long-haired man dressed in *sans culottes* and a none too clean shirt enters with food: a bowl of milk, a hunk of stale bread and a piece of mouldy cheese. He sets these down at the door, and before she can reach her meal, two enormous grey rats dash from the shadows to devour the bread and cheese. She seizes the bowl and drinks the milk, which is on the turn.

She hammers on the door. 'Let me out of here! There are rats, and they've eaten my food! Where's my brother?'

Nobody comes. She listens for footsteps, but there are none.

Chapter Thirty-Seven

Rumour and intrigue foment in the city. The decrees of August keep the Assembly busy with debate, and Mirabeau and Necker, who move between the Assembly and the Court, desperately try to prevent the King using his veto to deny The Rights of Man and the Citizen. Although Artois and Conde have fled, they correspond with Louis VXI who still has his wife expressing their opinions on their behalf.

The Duc d'Orleans and Marquis de Huruge argue for a march on Versailles to force the King to agree to the Assembly's recommendations, but throughout September delay after delay makes it seem unlikely.

Jacques's task, other than being a glorified paperboy, distributing not only Marat's newspaper, but also that of Desmoulins, is to talk about the cost-of-living crisis and to stir up discontent. Back in April, some factory owners found their premises and their homes burned to the ground when they talked of lowering wages, and there were rumours of crops being burned to keep the price of bread high.

He's seldom needed to worry about the price of food— Le Maitre keeps a good table, and there always seems to be money to pay for their meals—but in the conversations he has with the people in the markets, who often club together to buy an issue of the papers, which he knows will be shared among a dozen of them, he knows that almost half a worker's pay will be spent on the daily bread that is their staple diet, much as oatmeal is to the Scots and the potato is to the Irish.

Returning from the markets, he looks up at the attics where his sister is a prisoner. He recalls how much she fears rats. He told Suzanne and Le Maitre how she screamed at the sight of them in Scotland. She will crack soon, he has no doubt, and tell them where Ottilie is concealed. His gaze shifts to the floor below the attics, where strains of music flow from the violin of Gianfranco Valenti. The man asks for his wife and child constantly. 'Surely,' Jacques suggests, 'since we know where Lucette is, we could snatch the girl and they could be together?'

Le Maitre gives him a pitying look. 'As far as the girl knows, she is the daughter of the couple who brought her up. Nobody has told her any different. Leave her where she is until they need to bring her here.'

He looks to Suzanne for support. She nods her approval.

Jacques is all too aware that Suzanne spends her nights with Le Maitre, these days. Her husband is usually elsewhere in Paris with the handsome young deputy who is his constant companion.

Jacques' room is above Le Maitre's and the noises of their violent lovemaking keep him awake at night. They are like alley cats, he thinks, hearing their blood curdling screams and growls. He misses Suzanne's attentions, but sometimes his thoughts drift to Lucette, young, pretty and innocent.

Instead of going inside, Jacques turns to an inn for some company. A small group of Lafayette's National Guardsmen occupy the corner, with several jugs of red wine, and one of them, whom Jacques recognises, invites him to join them.

The King's army, many of whom fought in America, have been anything but loyal of late, and these men are full of rage that the Regiment of Flanders has been summoned by the Minister for War, the Comte de Saint Priest to strengthen the Hundred Swiss and Garde du Corps at the palace of Versailles. The regiment's officers are known to be less than sympathetic to the Assembly.

'They'll arrive at the end of the month. Watch out—the King will use them to try to shut the Assembly down.'

This is intelligence that Le Maitre will find useful. Jacques toasts his hosts and excuses himself to report back.

Le Maitre is on his way up the stairs, when he reaches the house. 'Your sister is a troublemaker. She's been screaming her head off upstairs, and we're still no closer to finding Valenti's wife.'

Jacques tells his news and is rewarded with a pat on the shoulder and an instruction to befriend the soldiers. He collects a tallow candle, lighting it from the candles in the hall, and mounts the stairs. In his own little room, he hangs his jacket on the peg behind the door, strips off the *sans culottes* and shirt and throws himself on the narrow bed.

Soon, the noise of Suzanne and Le Maitre's violent amours reach him. He picks up his own copy of today's pamphlet. Politics will be his bedfellow tonight.

Chapter Thirty-Eight

October 5th, 1789

Any day when bread is in short supply is a bad day for the women of Saint Antoine district, but today, when a loaf costs not half but all the money in their purses, something snaps.

The day is cold and grey, and ominous clouds block out the sun. There's a storm coming.

Nobody knows the name of the girl with the drum who starts things off, but one after another, they fall in step. This is what Jacques and Le Maitre have been waiting for—the call to action. He joins the march to the church. They are looking for places to meet and protest. Their first destination is the nearest church, which they know has a fine belltower. It's the work of a moment for him to slip inside and tell the bellringers the women want the bells to toll.

Soon the bells in every church in Paris are sounding the tocsin, and Jeannie, in her attic, looking out, sees in the marketplace below, women of all ages and a handful of men crowding in. Some of them are brandishing kitchen knives and rolling pins. At first, she thinks they are angry housewives setting out to punish their errant husbands, but then she sees Le Maitre and her brother leaping onto a table and shouting they are going to the Hotel de Ville—to make their demands for food.

The door opens, and Suzanne Gregory crosses to the window. She is carrying the dress from Jeannie's trunk. 'Put this on. You're coming with me.'

Jeannie hesitates, for a few seconds. 'Do you prefer to remain locked up with the rats, you silly girl?'

If she does as the woman demands, there is just a chance she might give her captors the slip, but Suzanne snaps, 'Don't even think of it.' The knife in the woman's hands is a slim poniard, 'I've killed before, and I've maimed. If you know what is good for you, you will do as you are told.'

There is no choice.

Suzanne holds the knife to Jeannie's back as they fall in with the crowds surging to the Hotel de Ville. The sour smell of sweat mingles with adrenalin. Jeannie thinks of a pack of hounds with blood in their nostrils, chasing down their quarry.

Behind them, violin in hand, marches Gianfranco Valenti. Everyone from the household is in the procession. There is nobody left to guard the prisoner of the Bastille, and Suzanne knows he will be useful to them.

At the head of the column, Jacques and Le Maitre have given way to the man who led the storming of the Bastille, Stanislas Maillard. He's a soldier with the National Guard. He makes their demands for food—and adds a further demand for weapons and ammunition.

Jostled, pushed along, bruised and hardly able to breathe, Jeannie is carried on the wave of anger and hunger, into the Hotel de Ville.

She watches the crowd seize the quartermaster, and string him up to a lamp post. 'What did he do?' she breathes.

Julie MP Adams

Her tormentor says, 'He tried to stop them getting the weapons.' but even as she speaks, Maillard orders them to cut the quartermaster down and let him go. He doesn't stop the mob from ransacking the building, but when some women want to burn it to the ground, he reminds them that if the day goes well, they will need the Town Hall when they return as the rulers of Paris.

Someone thrusts a hunk of bread and a lump of butter into her hands and Jeannie devours it gratefully. She's had days on end of little food, and she's faint with hunger. In that regard, she understands the anger of the mob.

Two women in front of her are draping tapestries taken from the building around them, in place of shawls. Others have taken carving knives and forks as weapons, and almost everyone seems to have a souvenir of this, first, triumph.

Maillard knows many of the women in the crowd by name and he chooses half a dozen and tells them to rally the people they know from their markets, and to form columns. They are marching 'To Versailles!'

Outside the rain has started, and within minutes, Jeannie is soaked to the skin. Suzanne's hands dig into her elbows, but at least she's sheathed the knife—for the moment.

There are rumours. Maillard's a member of the National Guard, and they're assembling at the Place de Greve.

Le Maitre orders Jacques to fall back and to join the soldiers. 'If any of them look like turning back, just tell them about what happened at that dinner.

A few nights before, when the Regiment of Flanders arrived at Versailles, there was a banquet in their honour. The soldiers removed the tricolour cockades from their hats and replaced them with the white cockade of the Bourbons. 'Tell them that the Flanders scum stamped on our badge.'

'What about Lafayette? He won't let them march against the King,' Jacques says.

The Scottish Agent

'If he hasn't been able to stop them up until now, then he'll be looking for a way to slow them down. He's probably sending someone ahead to warn them we're coming. Maillard has a message for them. If he betrays them, or turns them back to Paris, they're to kill him.'

'Their commander? The hero of the American wars?'

'Nobody is above the will of the Revolution.'

Lafayette, on horseback, looks grim. The municipal government of Paris tells him to bring the King back to Paris. 'If he won't come willingly, you'll need to arrest him and bring him by force. That's a mob out there that tore down the strongest prison in Paris with their bare hands. Do you think they will stop at regicide?'

The mob want food, but they want affordable food, every day. They want an end to rising prices. They want the Assembly to meet in Paris, where they won't be seduced by the luxuries of the Court. Above all, they want the King, in Paris, where he is visible—not hiding in a palace miles away. They talk kindly of the King, but at the mention of the Queen, they spit on the ground.

They set out on their journey, ten thousand strong, with the women at the front. Along the way they call to passers-by to fall in and march with them. In the middle of the procession, smaller canons from the Hotel de Ville are hauled by the marchers. Setting off mid-afternoon, with Lafayette at the head of their forces, come the fifteen thousand members of the National Guard.

Jeannie, marching with them, is constantly aware of Suzanne at her back. 'You're going to tell me what I want—or I may just allow myself to stumble and accidentally drive this knife through your miserable little heart.'

'I don't know what you are talking about,' she says, and tries to quicken her pace.

'Your brother was my lover, you silly girl. Le Maitre told

me to seduce him, to recruit him to our cause. He was more than willing to tell us everything he knows about your employer—and his work for the British. He didn't tell us quite everything—you had Le Maitre fooled into thinking you were a boy. When Jacques let slip that his twin was a girl, I suspected you might come in useful.'

'What did that old nun tell you about Ottilie? Where have they put her? What have they done with her?'

Jeannie considers her options. Can she seize the knife from Suzanne? How easy would it be to slip to the edge of the march? And is there anybody prepared to lift a finger to help her? If they march to the Assembly, can she throw herself on the mercy of Jacob Rose?

CHAPTER THIRTY-NINE

Lafayette's man, riding like the wind, reaches Versailles hours before the women's march, dropping from his horse and going straight to the presence of the King who is giving an audience to several members of the Assembly.

Messengers are sent to the Assembly, and to Trianon, to warn of impending danger. A force of over twenty-five thousand, even if half the number are women, is a serious threat. The messenger tells those with the King that Lafayette is a hostage rather than a commander. There is consternation.

'How long until they reach the palace?' asks the King.

'Several hours, Sire. They were four miles behind me, by my reckoning.'

'What are their demands?' Mirabeau asks. He has little time to address the members before the women arrive.

'They were angry about food, and the price of bread today, and they want the foreign regiments sent away and replaced with the National Guard. When I set out, there was talk of the Assembly and the Court moving to Paris.'

They exchange glances. The King looks up at the portrait

of Louis XIV and sighs. If he gives in to the marchers, he is betraying his ancestors. If he does not, it will result in war, and France, already on its knees, will be utterly doomed.

The messengers reach the Hameau, and there is consternation as the Queen's carriage leaves for the palace. She must be by the King's side. The farmer dashes out to secure the livestock. A ready supply of food will be too much for the marchers to resist.

Lucette, staring out of her window, is surprised by the farmer's wife, unlocking the door and gesturing to her to come out of the attic. 'There's trouble coming. You want to go to your parents?' she hisses.

The girl nods.

'There was a man here. Did you hear him say they are servants in the town? Mercier's household?'

She thrusts a bundle into Lucette's arms. 'The dress. It's caused nothing but trouble. Take it and go.'

Hesitating on the threshold, watching the heavy rain turn the courtyard to mud, Lucette thanks the woman, and hastens on the track that leads to the town. She remembers the road the farmer took with the horse and cart, but on foot it takes over an hour, in the rain and the mud. All she can think about, is seeing Papa Jules and Maman.

There is consternation in the town. Chanting coming from the road to Paris is heard. For a moment, Lucette is almost hypnotised by it. There are strains of music, a fiddle playing an unfamiliar air. She shakes off the notion and goes in search of Mercier's premises.

The shopkeepers are putting up shutters, and she stumbles into the square and into the arms of Jules.

'Papa, forgive me.'

He wants to fold her in his arms and weep over his lost child, but he grabs her arm and hauls her to the back door, pushing her over the threshold, before he goes to secure the

The Scottish Agent

stables. Who knows what danger is close to hand.

Chapter Forty

Wet and exhausted, the marchers should be miserable. They remain resolute. Jeannie's feet are blistered and there is a hole in the sole of her shoe. Suzanne does not give her leave to stop to examine the damage, shoving her viciously if she slows down.

They've arrived at the door of the Assembly, and looking at her tormentor's face, Jeannie is convinced that Suzanne is mad.

There are even more protestors with them now. Another force, learning of the march—country people from the surrounding area, has joined the bedraggled women of Paris. These marchers are armed with scythes and pitchforks and give the impression of knowing how to use them.

Miracle of miracles, Jacob Rose stands with Mirabeau and a young man in sombre clothes at the door. They invite Maillard, at the head of the column to enter and speak with the Assembly. They assure him there are no soldiers in the meeting hall. They are about to close the doors behind Maillard, but he insists they remain open.

Maillard argues the case against the Flanders Regiment

and passionately denounces the food prices that sparked the march this morning. The Assembly hear him, and at his desk at the front, Jacob Rose writes his record of their demands.

The women have been pushing against the heavy door, and some of them have entered the Assembly. A girl in front of Jeannie, worn out, sinks exhausted onto a bench beside the deputies. She tells the man beside her that she has not eaten for two days. Willpower alone carried her on the six-hour forced march from Paris.

The women at the door demand to hear from Mirabeau. He declines, instead, moving among them, speaking to them kindly, asking about their families. It is young Maximilian Robespierre who rises to the occasion, taking the women's part: pleading their cause to the Assembly.

The women may be almost too tired to move, but the swiftness of the march and its organisation terrify the deputies. These people could turn on them. Mirabeau offers up a silent prayer of thanks for young Robespierre's intervention. His words turned the anger of the women. He might just have saved the lives of every Assembly member present tonight.

At the door of the hall, a tired man raises his violin to his chin and plays an encouraging air. The deputies turn to listen, and Suzanne Gregory leaps up and applauds the musician— 'A Prisoner of the Bastille.'

The moment of triumph should be enough for Jeannie to break free, and she runs towards where Jacob perches at his desk. She is so near, but a hand reaches out and grabs her by the waist. 'Not so fast, sister. You'll do as I say. Tell me where to find Valenti's wife.'

Chapter Forty-One

Jacob turns his head but not in time to see Jeannie dragged off by her twin. Johnny, or Jacques, as he chooses to be called, drags her outside the door of the meeting hall, a hand over her mouth to stop her screaming. She struggles and manages to land a few kicks on his shins, but the remains of her shoes are not hard enough to do much harm.

She watches as Maillard gathers up the leaders of his columns: women from each of six Parisian markets. The Assembly president, Jean Joseph Mounier, is going to present them to the King, where they can make their demands. The women stand up a little straighter and try to adjust their bedraggled appearance, and the small procession goes to the Palace.

This does not please Le Maitre, or his disciples. The Royal Guards have the marchers contained in the square, and Lafayette's National Guard has taken its time following the women. 'He's playing for time,' Le Maitre snarls.

The deputation returns, with the news that food will be given out. The King listened to their demands and when one of the women fainted, more likely from hunger than from being overwhelmed by meeting royalty, he declared himself sympathetic to their plight. Maillard is already talking about turning back to Paris—the last thing that Suzanne wants. 'They want to go back? Just when we can force Louis and his wretched wife to their knees? I do not believe the cheek of that man!'

Le Maitre and Suzanne move around the crowd, encouraging them to leave the Assembly hall and to move closer to the palace. They suggest that the King's word cannot be trusted—that Marie Antoinette will get him to go back on any promises he makes.

At six o clock that evening, the King gathers his advisers together. They counsel him that he is in grave danger and reluctantly he announces that he will accept the August decrees and the Declaration of the Rights of Man without any changes. The Royal Guards have orders to fall back to the palace grounds. Only the sixty or so Gardes de Corps are posted around the palace to guard the King.

Lafayette arrives with the National Guard hours later, marching up the Avenue de Paris and, leaving his men behind, reports to the King. 'No doubt grovelling at his feet, the miserable fool,' Suzanne snaps.

Unlike the Royal Guard, who had stood firm in the square, neither attacking the women nor showing any favour, the National Guardsmen join the marchers at the gates, sharing rations and seeking out friends from the city. Jeannie, still forced to stand near her twin, gratefully takes a drink from a guardsman's flask of watered wine. 'What's happening?' she manages to ask, out of earshot of her brother and his friends.

'They're saying Lafayette is a traitor,' he replies.

'Is that what you think?' she asks.

'I fought with him in America. He was brave enough there, but he's an aristocrat, and most of them won't dare act against the King. If he betrays us, he will be dead by morning. There's enough of us to make that happen.'

Jeannie tries to edge through the crowd, but time and again, either her brother or Suzanne drag her back. 'Why do you need me?' she wails. 'I'm of no use to you now. Let me go!'

'It's where you go that bothers me,' Suzanne hisses. 'Straight to Jacob Rose to report your own brother as an agent provocateur? No, I have work for you to do.'

The soldiers and the women, together with the men from the area who joined the march, drift towards the Palace. The gates are closed, but not all of them have a guard posted.

At six o clock in the morning, when it is still dark, Jacques shakes his sister awake from where she had slumped against a side gate. He's fiddling with something in the lock, and he pushes the gate open. The crowds—seeing a way in, swarm through the opening, pushing Jeannie aside.

She rubs the sleep from her eyes, wishing she had stayed in the dream where she was Jean the clerk, walking to the bakery for the daily bread, without a care in the world. Jacques grabs her arm and drags her with him. Through the unguarded gate, they go, following the crowds who now swarm round the palace, seeking a way into the building, and finding it. The guards fire at the intruders and a girl falls to the ground dead. The crowd press on, determined to avenge their martyr.

Suzanne, dagger drawn, demands to know the way to the Queen's bedchamber, and those with her are baying for blood. Through the gilded corridors they go, slashing at tapestries, overturning furniture, a tidal wave of destruction. When a guard confronts them, Jeannie sees the young man is trembling with fear, but equally scared of the consequences of not doing his duty.

They strike him down, and to Jeanne's horror, they strike

The Scottish Agent

off his head with a scythe, and put it on his own pike, raising it aloft. A second guard is badly hurt, but they walk over him on their way to the Queen's apartment.

There they bang on the doors, hammering with fists, shouting their rage, all the while egged on by Suzanne, who roars 'Death to the Queen!' Pressed up against the door, despite the roaring of those around her, Jeannie can hear a scuffle—the Queen and her ladies are leaving by another exit.

Suzanne continues to bang at the door, but Jacques, using his skeleton key all the while, picks the lock and the doors fly open, to reveal a dishevelled bed, and the open door to the corridor leading to the King's private apartments. They can hear footsteps in the distance and hammering as the queen and her ladies demand to be let in. Suzanne races down the corridor, only to have the door slammed in her face.

Denied their quarry, the women attack the gilded bed, tearing down the curtains, ripping the fine linen sheets and slashing the goose feather pillows. The room is swiftly full of rags, tatters and feathers. Suzanne collapses onto the floor, screaming with frustrated rage, and Jeannie gives a silent prayer of thanks that it took her brother the few extra seconds to pick the lock—moments that delivered Marie Antoinette into her husband's arms.

Chapter Forty-Two

Jacob has not slept properly. When the intruders left the Assembly meeting hall, he put his papers in the folder and walked with Henriette's husband to the house, where the doors were firmly locked and only opened momentarily to admit the two men, before the servants at the door fastened them and bolted them.

He's worked through the night, snatching only an hour of sleep when his eyelids would not stay open and he stumbled to the bed.

At daybreak, the house is woken by a furious knocking.

There's panic as a messenger tells his host that the mob have entered the Royal quarters. Lafayette, asleep in his house in the town has been alerted and is on his way to the palace on foot, to take charge of the chaos.

Jacob knows he must summon a meeting of the Assembly and returns to his room to splash water on his face and gather his papers, before snatching a breakfast cup from the dining room.

Lafayette's orders have cleared the mob from the palace. They are gathering in the square outside the Assembly and their mood remains angry. Mirabeau greets Jacob and says that they must go to the Palace. 'I've told Lafayette to remain close to the King. He says that even the Flanders Regiment are refusing to attack these people, and he's sending the Royal guard to Rambouillet until they're needed.'

'How is he going to deal with this?' Jacob asks. He remembers Jean the clerk's report of that first demonstration. This mob are not afraid of any consequences of their violent actions. He tightens his grip on his cane.

'He will get the King to make an appearance on the balcony and accept the will of the people.'

'Which is?'

'He's going to tell the King and Queen they must pack. They'll be moved to Paris this afternoon.'

'And return when?' Versailles has been the seat of power for over a hundred and fifty years. It was the creation of Louis XIV—putting distance between the King and the people—and with the nobles kept close, it minimised any attempt at a coup by them. That Louis, however, didn't consider that an angry, hungry peasantry might pose a significant threat.

'Sometime, perhaps never,' the statesman replies. 'It looks as if you too will have your wish. Our Assembly will follow the King to Paris. Tonight, you will sleep in your own bed.

Lafayette plays his part to perfection, presenting the King to his people, to address 'My good and faithful subjects' with the news that he will go with them to Paris this very day. Lafayette pins a tricolor cockade on the guards on the balcony and a cheer rises from the mob below.

It's not over. A shrill voice from the crowd demands the Queen appears also. There's a moment's hesitation before Lafayette conducts Marie Antoinette and her children onto the balcony. Where there was cheering for the King, the women boo her. 'Why's she hiding behind her children?' one of them screams. 'Take them away, so we can get at her!'

The frightened little boy and girl are called inside, and Marie Antoinette stands, her hands at her bosom in prayer. Lafayette, knowing that even he is not safe from the wrath of the mob, takes a calculated risk, kneels and kisses the Queen's hand. Jacob and Mirabeau shout 'God Save the Queen!' and thankfully their words are echoed by others in the crowd.

They walk through the people, many of whom are seeing the palace in daylight for the first time in their lives, shocked by its grandeur, scale and wealth. The masterpiece of Le Vaux, Le Notre and Le Brun—and the dream of a Sun King who will no doubt, this day, be rolling in his tomb at its abandonment.

At one o clock, the procession, now sixty thousand strong, led by the National Guard, sets out for Paris, with the King and Queen, their children and the Court in the carriages slowly progressing towards Paris. There's almost a festive atmosphere. The crowd, drunk on their triumph, ride on the captured guns from yesterday, and Jacob, following with the deputies, tired but determined, is shocked that alongside the carriages, marchers hold aloft on pikes the heads of the slaughtered royal guards.

It takes nine terrifying hours for the march to reach Paris, and when the King on arrival at the Tuileries is asked by his major domo what his orders are, he shrugs, and says that 'every man should put himself wherever he pleases.' The Tuileries have not been a royal residence for so long, there are no longer official state bedchambers.

Jacob and Mirabeau learn he called for wine, and a copy of 'The Life of Charles I.' Jacob shudders at the choice of reading. A beheaded king? Who would countenance that in France?

Chapter Forty-Three

Jeannie watches the procession depart. Suzanne and Le Maitre, along with her husband, go with them, leaving her behind with her brother. It's a small mercy but an uncertain one. Jeannie doesn't know the man that her twin has become. She doesn't feel safe with him.

They are both worn out. Jeannie's feet are blistered and bleeding and she hasn't eaten for a long time. She sinks to the ground and refuses to move. If he wants her to go anywhere, he must carry her. He has a task to complete, but Suzanne has ordered him to always keep her in his sight. He shrugs, then puts an arm around her and half drags her several streets away to a town house. He bangs on the door, and when there is no reply, he pulls the skeleton key from his pocket and fiddles with the lock. The door swings open and he puts a finger to his lips and ushers her inside.

They mount the stairs to the bedroom where he slept with Suzanne, and she stumbles to the bed and collapses on it.

Jacques has a moment's remorse. It is his sister lying face down on that bed, exhausted and in a state of shock at the violence she has witnessed. What he must do, however, cannot wait. He closes the door softly and leaves the house.

The town of Versailles is ravaged and in tatters. The market stalls are overturned, the taverns closed and the houses shuttered. Many of the occupants, deputies, are on their way to Paris. Others—the aristocrats—are frantically packing to leave not only Versailles, but France. It's obvious the King is no longer in charge, and they are looking to save their own fortunes.

The livery stables are empty of horses and grooms and he must walk to Trianon.

He arrived in Paris just over a year ago, an impetuous young student, dreaming of escaping to a new life in America. Now, he's a driving force of the Revolution—an *agent provocateur*. Much of what has happened over the last two days has been as much down to his instigation as it's been due to the hordes of hungry harridans howling for blood at the price of bread. He's worked his harm in those marketplaces for months now, stirring up ill feeling, handing out those pamphlets and journals.

Why does he feel cheated? Suzanne has discarded him for Le Maitre, who he suspects is cheating Marat by accepting payment from the Duc d'Orléans. Yet the siren still has a hold over him.

The rain that blighted the past few days has stopped and the sun makes a feeble attempt to part the clouds. He passes farms where only children are left to tend the livestock, as the workers joined the march to Paris. He stops at one smallholding to ask for something to eat, offering a handful of *sous* in exchange for an apple and a hunk of bread and butter. The little girl who brings his food shyly points him in the direction of the Hameau.

The sadness of the little place surprises him. The hamlet is silent and there is little activity. The Queen, a prisoner in her gilded carriage, heading to the Tuileries might never come here again. He walks past the tiny lake and stands below the Queen's House.

The shadow appearing alongside his own indicates he is not alone. A sullen faced girl with a birthmark on her cheek is looking at him from head to foot.

He assumes his most winning smile. 'Where is Lucette? I've been sent to collect her. Her father needs her.'

The girl makes a sound that is neither a laugh nor a cough, 'You'll be that young man we were warned about. The one that grand lady said was out to seduce her. Farmer had her locked up in the attic, but his wife panicked when that Deputy turned up, asking for her. She let her go, yesterday.'

This is not the news he expected. He was to collect Lucette and to get his sister to lead them to Ottilie. Suzanne's plan depends on this, and if he fails, she will make him suffer.

'Where did she go?'

The dour farmer appears, clutching a pitchfork and growls, 'None of your business.' A dog behind him growls. At the window of the cottage, the farmer's wife stands, holding a hand to a bruised face.

Jacques does not wish to admit defeat or return to Paris without his task completed. The only person who can help him is his twin, and she will require persuasion. She had Suzanne's knife at her back all day yesterday—and did not give in to her. Perhaps he needs to try a different sort of coaxing? He saw her frustration at being stopped from throwing herself at Jacob Rose.

He returns to the town in low spirits, exhausted and annoyed. In the house, he goes to the cellar to collect a bottle of brandy and drinks a large measure. He's entitled to Monsieur Gregory's hospitality, if nothing else. The warmth hits his empty belly, warming it, and ridding his mind of anxiety. He helps himself to another measure, and another.

Mellowed by the spirits, he climbs the stairs to find his sister sleeping. He strips off his jacket and trousers, throws himself down on the bed beside her and as the sun sinks, casting shadows across the room, he abandons any resistance and falls into a deep uneasy slumber.

Chapter Forty-Four

Jeannie wakes in the night, and slips from the bed, to use the commode. Her brother is still fast asleep, snoring heavily and she smells the brandy on his breath. She tiptoes from the bedchamber. The house is empty of its occupants, and she goes from room to room, until in the kitchen she finds the remnants of a stale loaf and a cold roasted chicken. There's a half empty bottle of wine, and she sits at the kitchen table to eat, forcing herself to chew each mouthful to avoid making herself sick.

She tries to shut out the horrors of the day before—if she thinks of the decapitated guards, it will drive her mad. She can still hear Suzanne Gregory howling for the blood of the queen and see her take out her rage on the bed. The woman is evil, insane or both.

The room is lit only by the moon outside. She needs to think carefully about what to do next. When she left the convent, she was convinced that she must conceal Ottilie's refuge from her brother and the woman that controls him. She needs to get to Jacob and confess the truth about the bargain she made with her brother. Then she can tell him where to find Ottilie and ask him to find her employment. Perhaps Sandy Geddes can help?

At all costs she needs to get out of this house without her brother following. She tiptoes up the stairs and into the bedchamber. Holding her breath, she collects her brother's clothes and his shoes—a size too large for her and returns to the kitchen where she discards her dress and stays and tends to her poor, hurt feet.

Minutes later, her hair plaited and clubbed, dressed once more in boy's clothing, and walking in the shadows, she makes her way to the house where Jacob Rose has been staying these last few months. She avoids the front door, skirting round the building to the servant's quarters. It's early daylight and there are signs of life at the kitchen window.

The scullery maid tells the ruffianly *sans culotte* that Jacob Rose has gone to Paris, with the deputies following the procession. Jeannie turns to walk, and the servant tells her that they're sending a cart to collect Jacob's possessions. She's in luck—she'll have a ride to the city.

It is almost noon when Jacques wakes from his drunken slumber. His head aches, and he tries to turn over, shutting out the dazzling midday sunlight that makes the room unbearably bright for his hungover eyes. His mouth is dry. He needs water. He stumbles to the commode, and relieves himself, before reaching for the jug that stands full on the washstand.

It takes several moments for the truth to sink in. There's something missing. Jeannie is gone, and so are his clothes and shoes. He groans. First Lucette disappears and now his sister is goodness knows where, dressed as him. Clad only in his shirt, he goes downstairs. In the kitchen, he finds the remnants of her repast. Her dress, stained with the blood of the dead guards, is stuffed into the fireplace, and her shoes, with the sole beyond repair are discarded under the kitchen table.

He cannot leave the house in his shirt, and on no account does he plan to wear his sister's dress. His stomach heaves from last night's drinking and he dashes to the scullery to vomit into a bucket.

Head aching, he returns to the bedroom. There is clothing belonging to Suzanne's husband—a taller and broader man—of the quality worn at court. He groans and falls back into the bed.

Chapter Forty-Five

He's missed the little house and its small comforts, but on the seventh of October, after the ordeals of the journey to Paris, when he needed to shut out the sight of the heads waved around on pikes, he finds he cannot settle, and after a meagre breakfast he walks to visit Sandy Geddes.

Geddes and his wife remained in Paris when Jacob returned to Versailles, and they demand an account of the past two days. He obliges, and when he tries to offer testimony that leaves out the worst of the violence, Francine says, 'All of it, please. Jacob, if you don't talk about what you saw, it will drive you mad.'

She orders the servants to bring tea, and they sit in her bright parlour, on spindly legged chairs, talking of the horrors that he cannot drive from his mind.

He tells of going to the Palace with Mirabeau and seeing the wreckage of the royal apartments, and the corpses of the brave men who tried to defend the King and Queen, paying for the privilege with their lives—and their heads. Finally, he tells of the disarray of the arrival at the Tuileries and the king's choice of book. 'It's as if he fully expects to meet his end on the executioner's block,' he says. He thinks of a conversation with Deputy Guillotin, recently, who asked him about that Scottish means of beheading—the Maiden, and how it might be modified to deliver a swift end, and he shudders.

Sandy listens, his countenance grim. Francine asks, 'How did it come to this?'

'There's been talk of agents of the Duc D'Orléans stirring up the crowd. He's told the likes of Desmoulins that Louis will never stand for being a constitutional monarch and that he'd be a more suitable replacement if the king is exiled,' Jacob tells them. 'The printer that calls himself Le Maitre, appears to be behind those agents. I fear he's in league with Marat—and I've seen the lad that must be Johnny Rose with them.'

Francine says, 'Can nobody call them to account?'

Jacob shakes his head and raises his teacup to his lips. He drinks, and for a moment is silent. 'The soldiers flatly refused to fire on the mob. It's as if they no longer serve the king. In the Assembly, the women swarmed in like flies, sitting on the benches. They all carried knives, and we owed our lives to young Robespierre. He somehow managed to calm things over, long enough to move them from the building.'

Sandy goes to the table where a clay pipe rests on a stand, with a humidor of tobacco. He takes his time over filling it, tamping it down and lighting it. He takes several puffs, blowing smoke rings, to his wife's annoyance.

'If Maximilian Robespierre is acceptable to the mob, then we are all finished,' he says. 'The man keeps company with that agitator Desmoulins, and the thug Danton. Yes, Jacob, I know they are lawyers, but if they can make the mob dance to their tune, then who is to keep the law?'

Jacob falls silent. The orders from Britain warned precisely of this situation, and it has gone beyond his control.

'We need a spy in their midst. Someone who can tell what their next movement will be. It would need to be someone that they trust, who they would never suspect of betraying them.'

'Someone who could move freely among them, and report to you when they plan another attack, like the Bastille?' Geddes asks.

A thought has seeded itself in Jacob's mind and begun to take root. 'The twins. We need to find Jean as a matter of urgency. Yes, I think that might just do.'

'A girl?' Doubt is written on Sandy's face, but Francine nods.

'She lived as a boy for months, without you suspecting, Jacob. You said that the nuns at Passy and Longchamps trusted her. It could work, if you could find her. What about her brother?'

'He might prove more of a challenge,' Jacob agrees, 'unless we have something to hold over him? What do you know of his past, Sandy?'

'Enough to know he left Scotland as a felon, who otherwise was bound for Australia. I can write to Kilravock.'

The clock chimes eleven and Jacob rises. 'My hosts are sending on my box and my papers. The cart will deliver them around noon. I must take my leave of you.'

Sandy shakes hands, giving a Masonic squeeze, and is rewarded with a faint smile. Francine rises and kisses him on both cheeks.

He walks to his house, hand tightening on the cane, and arrives as the cart draws up at the door and a young man in short jacket and *sans culottes* drops from the passenger seat, reaching up to receive the box. He thanks the carter, who shakes the reins and moves off.

Jacob unlocks the door and stands aside for the delivery lad.

The Scottish Agent

'Monsieur Rose—I'm home, if you'll have me,' says Jean the clerk.

Chapter Forty-Six

They are shy with one another; in a way they have not been before. As notary and clerk, they maintained a dignified distance, where each respected the other's need for privacy. Since the Assembly claimed Jacob's time, he's relied on his clerk, and lately he's sent her into danger. He feels responsible for her suffering, and he tells her so.

In return, she tells her story. She begins with the arrival of her stepmother and the twins' departure for Aberdeen and their tutor's home. She tells of her love of learning, and how the bargain she made with her twin, dressing as a lad and taking his place at the lectures was less about protecting him that it was about her passion for study.

Johnny took it for granted that his twin would always smooth things over for him, assuming she did so out of familial loyalty. He rewarded her by taking the little money they had, and drinking in bad company, finally committing a felony.

Jacob asks if it was a political crime that cost her brother his freedom? Sandy Geddes told him that Johnny was bound for the Penal Colony of Australia.

The Scottish Agent

'Had he been transported; I would have been bound to go with him. He is my only close kin, and after his crimes I could not remain at our tutor's home. His crimes were public affray, and theft. He was told that if we came here that it was on the understanding that neither of us could return to Scotland.

'I hoped that working for you, he would learn to behave with responsibility. I reconciled myself to being companion to Mistress Danby, having bed and board and a purpose. I forced him to behave well on the journey from Scotland, but when we arrived and found Mistress Danby's house closed and learned of her death, he told me he did not wish the life of a clerk and he had been writing to men like Marat, who would offer him work he would enjoy more. He used to try to visit while you were abroad, and I would pretend to be put upon, so he would not suspect I like my work, and take it from me. He takes everything that I love.'

There is sadness in her voice. She recounts her journeys to Passy and to Longchamps, and what she learned of Suzanne's past.

'There is a connection between Madame Gregory and the Countess de la Motte?' Jacob asks.

Jeannie nods. 'Also, both women, as girls, shared their lessons with Ottilie de Saint Combs, who is surely the birth mother of Lucette. It seems that they witnessed her marriage to the Queen's music master, and that Marie Antoinette was also present. She favoured Ottilie, and the other girls were so jealous that they betrayed Ottilie to her father and the man she was betrothed to.'

'Ottilie had her child taken, and her young husband thrown in the Bastille. He's been held a prisoner at the Gregory house, and she had Lucette locked up somewhere too.'

'I found Lucette, and returned her to Jules,' Jacob tells

her.

'Where is Ottilie now?' Jacob asks.

'She's in the asylum at Charenton. Suzanne beat me and locked me in a room with rats—my brother knows I fear them. She had my brother follow me to the convent, but I took care to tell him nothing. If Suzanne captures Ottilie as well, she plans to use them to cause even more trouble for the Queen.'

Remembering the trembling woman on the balcony, Jacob understands the clerk's silence. 'You did well. Now, we must act swiftly.'

Chapter Forty-Seven

They are neither of them sure what to expect at Charenton. Jeannie, still in her brother's clothes, has accounts of Bedlam in mind—the frightening place where men can dispose of inconvenient relatives by declaring them mad.

The superintendent greets the two men, 'Monsieur Rose? The Abbess of Longchamps has written to advise you wish to visit the patient known as Ottilie de Sant Combs.'

'Might we see her?' Jacob asks.

He leads them down a corridor, where cells at either side have a small window in the door, where the wardens may check on them.

'On this floor, our patients are melancholic,' he tells them. They reach the final cell where a woman in nun's clothing, rocks a cradle, where a swaddled doll looks blankly up at her.

'She misses her child,' he says. The nuns say that the girl's adoptive mother wrote several times a year, to tell of the child's progress. The letters ceased when the girl was sixteen, and from that moment on, Ottilie stopped eating or speaking. They sent her here, where we found that offering her a baby of sorts to care for, gives her a reason to stay in this world. She's found her voice again, since she has had this.'

Jacob says, 'The child is a grown young woman, and her father is recently released from the Bastille. If we brought them to see her, might that be beneficial to her?'

The man considers. 'We can try, but it might distress her even further. Perhaps we could prepare her, gradually?'

He taps on the door, unlocks it and opens it, to let them into the tiny room.

'Ottilie, you have visitors,' he says. 'I will wait outside. Do not raise your hopes.'

Jeannie sits on the narrow bed. 'Ottilie, we've got some news for you.'

The woman looks up and Jeannie is surprised to see Lucette's face, older, turned to hers. 'I've come from Lucette. Would you like to meet her? We can bring her to you.'

Ottilie reaches into the cradle and takes the doll in her arms, holding it to her bosom, and smiling up radiantly. 'Would you like to hold my daughter? Isn't she a lovely baby?' Jeannie reaches out for the doll and cradles it carefully.

Jacob says, 'Your daughter is a young woman. She's very beautiful. Might we bring her to see you?'

She snatches the doll back and clutches it to her, shaking her head and crying, 'No! No!'

The superintendent is at the door. 'She gets upset—telling her that the child is a woman, is a reminder of the years she has missed. I told you that this might upset her.'

He settles Ottilie, who is nursing the doll as he locks the cell and returns to the front door with them.

'There's a woman called Suzanne Gregory, or Madame Gregoire. She has Ottilie's husband in her custody, and she might bring him to see her. She arranged for the daughter, Lucette to be locked up and delivered to her. She believes that bringing them together might be used for political gain,' Jacob says. 'What would you advise?'

The superintendent shakes his head. 'Such a reunion would either bring great joy or would destroy the patient. If she sees her husband and the daughter together, without warning, she may assume the child is his lover, and that she is abandoned all over again. Try to reunite the father and daughter first but take great care.'

They leave Charenton and return to their hired carriage. Jeannie says, 'He's kind. I didn't expect that.'

'How was Valenti when you saw him at the Gregory house?' Jacob asks.

'He played his violin and asked for his wife and child. She forced him to go on the march, and it was his music you heard when we got to the Assembly. He's been in some sort of trance—he needs to play music constantly. I tried to reach you, but Johnny stopped me. I didn't see Valenti afterwards. We were too tired to go on the march back and I forced Johnny to let me sleep. He left me—I think he was supposed to try to find Lucette and on his return he got drunk. He was asleep when I took his clothes and went to Francine's brother in law's house.'

Jacob smiles, 'You are a very convincing lad, and an excellent agent. Now we must track down Valenti and your brother. We need to put a stop to Madame Gregory's plans.'

Chapter Forty-Eight

In the confusion of the attack on the Queen's chambers, nobody sees Gianfranco Valenti leave the mob and wander through the palace, violin and bow in hand. He's walked and walked, and his fingers are sore from playing. He's glad to be away from that house where he was taken after the Bastille. He's tired of that woman telling him he cannot see Ottilie.

The horrors he's witnessed since leaving his cell have left him unable to string thoughts together, but Versailles was his home once.

After twenty years, he remembers this place and its secret doors and closets. He makes his way to the room where he sat at the harpsichord with his future wife, and laying down the violin and bow, he opens the lid of the delicate instrument and starts to play a variation on the theme that has given him a reason to go on living.

When he is too tired to play, he lies on the couch and sleeps fitfully, waking to another day, with sunshine dancing on the mirrors of the music room. He raises himself from the couch, stretches and returns to the instrument, flexing his fingers and sounding out those precious notes that tell of love and loss and heartbreak.

Those courtiers and servants in the palace who did not flee, retreated into the secret places and only after they are sure that the procession has departed for Paris do they emerge. They face an uncertain future. They do not know if their masters will ever return to this place.

The keeper of the Queen's Music is one of those who steal from the shadows into the light, to find his mistress gone, and the great halls silent, but for the delicate music in a private chamber.

It has been twenty long years since Giuseppe Valenti set eyes on his son, whom he feared he would never see again. He listens for a while, and then goes to sit beside Gianfranco, taking up the bass notes. When they finish playing, he places his hand on his son's. 'Welcome back.'

***

In Paris, Gregory and his wife arrive back at their townhouse. Suzanne's husband, for once has decided to be masterful. The dishevelled harpy that the guards ejected from the palace, still screaming threats at the queen, was bundled into their carriage, still wearing the bloodstained clothing in which she attacked the Queen's bedchamber.

During the nine hours of confinement with her, as the carriage proceeds at a snail's pace in the procession, she screams vile insults at him. She's lost sight of the Italian musician, and he's glad not to put up with the constant music. He's never liked violins.

She rages about Jacques and his failure to find Ottilie. She raves about a plan to discredit the Queen, like a mad woman.

Theirs has never been a conventional match. She's provided a cover for his true preferences—but now the Assembly is moving to Paris, he'd rather share his house with the young deputy from Lyons, than his wife and her obnoxious lover. Now that Le Maitre has served his purpose—getting the mob to show their strength so dramatically that the King accepts the end of the *Ancien Regime*, he's a mind to throw them out.

He considers options—divorce? Or perhaps, after her recent behaviour he might have her committed to an asylum?

***

It is several days and three bottles of cognac later when Jacques sufficiently recovers his wits to decide what to do next. His head still hurts and he's lost count of the times he has used the stinking chamber pot and the basin beside the bed.

Looking in the mirror, he sees the results of his dissipation—red eyes and a furred tongue. His teeth hurt too. He feels sick, but he must eat. Wrapping a sheet about him, he goes down to the kitchen. There is no sign of any servants and some stray animal has got in the window and devoured the remains of the chicken. The bread is hard as a rock, but he finds an egg, which he cracks into a cup and whisks with a fork, before swallowing it raw. It refuses to stay down. He must find clothing, and go in search of food, and something he can use to pay for it. Jeannie has taken his jacket and trousers, along with the money he had in his pocket.

Gregory's clothes are too big for him, but he finds a pair of knee breeches, and some silk stockings, which he puts on. His shirt is stained with sweat and goodness knows what, so he washes with the brackish water from the ewer, and helps himself to a fine lawn one, five sizes too large and a lace edged stock to go with it. A fine dark blue wool coat completes the ensemble, but the shoes in the closet are too large. He hunts around and finds a pair of Suzanne Gregory's riding boots, which he can squeeze his feet into, if they are too tight for comfort. He thinks of a line from a play about ill-fitting clothes. Which play was it and what was the significance?

If he is to eat, he will need money. He looks in the pockets of the clothes and in the drawers of the bureau and finds two gold *livres* and a few *sous*. He helps himself to some of Suzanne's trinkets—a locket containing a miniature portrait and a large paste and enamelled brooch. He tidies his hair with Gregory's comb, pocketing it, and with a final look at the dishevelled room, he turns on his heel and leaves the house.

He has failed Suzanne. His sister has escaped; he's lost Lucette and now he realises, the last time he saw Valenti was in the Queen's Bedchamber. As for Le Maitre? He's done with them.

The town of Versailles is stirring. The court may be moving away, but life must go on for the townsfolk. The shutters have been removed from the shops, and the stalls are set up in the square once more. It is quieter than usual, and he watches as a carriage, heavily laden with luggage groans off in the opposite direction to Paris.

At an inn, he spends some of his coin on a bowl of soup, a hunk of bread and some charcuterie with cheese. This, his stomach tolerates, but he waters his wine, to be on the safe side. He toys with the idea of walking to Paris, but asks the innkeeper if any carter might take a passenger in exchange for help with loading? The man looks at his expensive, ill-fitting clothes with suspicion, but sends him across the square to where a cart will take vegetables to Paris.

He doesn't notice Lucette, sweeping the street outside Mercier's, singing softly to herself as she works, or her father, washing the shop window, glad to have his family restored.

Chapter Forty-Nine

Suzanne and Le Maitre, riding at speed from Paris, pass the cart bearing Jacques and baskets of onions and garlic towards Paris.

Her husband bundled her into their carriage yesterday, refusing to tell her where they were going, until they stopped outside Charenton asylum.

The superintendent came out to greet them. Realising her husband's intentions, she drew the knife she keeps in her garter, but he squeezed her hand so hard it dropped from her grasp.

'I need to commit my wife for her own safety,' her husband tells the man.

She looks up at the square building. From the top floor she hears a piercing scream. A nun, looking down from the window to the occupants of the carriage below is making that unearthly noise and she cannot for the life of her imagine why.

It's enough of a distraction for her to slip from Monsieur Gregory's grasp and take to her heels. She darts into a garden to hide, slipping through a gate into the next street and into a church where she covers her head and slips into the confessional. When after a fruitless search the carriage moves away, she steals through the side streets, until she is in Paris, close to where Le Maitre lodges.

If she remains in Paris, her husband is determined to commit her. As a deputy, he is respectable, and as her spouse he has the right to dispose of her. She will make her way to the house at Versailles, to collect her jewels. They will ride for Calais and take ship for England. Her plans for Ottilie and Valenti can wait. For the moment, the Queen is a prisoner in the Tuileries.

The Scottish Agent

Le Maitre, ejected from the Paris house, with his worldly goods in a small valise is at his old lodgings. She tells him her plan and they hire two horses and set out on the road, riding swiftly to put as much distance between themselves and Paris as possible, before her husband comes after them.

The door of the house is wide open. Her rooms are ransacked. The stained sheets on the bed, the stinking chamber pot and the empty brandy bottle show an intruder has been here. She looks for the box that contains her most important jewels—a miniature of her mother, and a diamond brooch containing stones from the Queen's necklace. They are not there.

Le Maitre, impatient to be off, hears her screams of frustration and rage, which echo to the streets below.

Acknowledgements

Several years ago, I was challenged to undertake a writing apprenticeship: several novels in different genres. The idea for this book has been around for a very long time. I love historical fiction, and this is intended to be the first book in a series featuring the Rose family, and in particular JA Rose. I came across him in a book I found after my grandmother's death, which mentioned him as attaining rank during the Revolution and saving lives during the Terror. The Electric Scotland website gives a little more detail and tells that he was an Usher in the Assembly, and that he played a part in the downfall of Robespierre. I wanted to explore how a Scot, living in Paris in the later 18th century would have become involved in politics, and become a friend of some very significant figures.

The Revolution was a topic I studied for Higher History at school, at a time when the subject involved much rote learning and while I can reel off the main events, I needed to find out much more about the human stories behind them. The late, great Hilary Mantel said that had the internet been in place when she wrote her own Revolution novel, 'A Place of Greater Safety' that it would have saved a great deal of time. I am indebted to the website for the palace of Versailles, and to the various timelines available on the internet, which gave links to essays that cite the key texts by Simon Schama and Thomas Carlyle.

Much of what is in this book is controversial. In the 18thC, women could only learn outside universities, and my character of Jean/Jeannie, looks at the dilemma of a girl who loves learning and the opportunities it can offer—if she can take the place of her twin brother. There are references to the slave trade, also, where Scotland played a more significant part than we feel comfortable with nowadays.

It is also worth exploring the role that the Scottish enlightenment played in both the French and American revolutions. One of the poetry books that arrive on JA Rose's desk would have included the first volume by Robert Burns, whose more radical verses, often took the form of songs.

In the next two volumes I want to explore the role of women revolutionaries like Madame Roland. I want to write more about young Etienne, and we certainly have not seen the back of Johnny/Jacques Rose or the villainous Suzanne.

My thanks, as always, go to Heather Osborne, who takes the manuscript and works magic, to allow me to self-publish on Amazon. I write the way other people knit, and my first readers—family and friends—will get their copies as Christmas gifts.

Finally, the book is dedicated to my late grandmother, Margaret, who along with my uncle James, took an interest in genealogy. The phrase, never did anyone do so much harm trying to do so much good, was levelled at her during one family row—she explained it as being a reference to JA Rose and the revolution.

About the Author

Julie Adams has lived most of her life in the North East of Scotland. A retired teacher, she enjoys writing, walking, reading, cinema and theatre. She is a walk leader and a volunteer tour guide.

Printed in Great Britain
by Amazon